THE FORTUNES OF TEXAS

*Follow the lives and loves of a complex family
with a rich history and deep ties
in the Lone Star State*

FORTUNE'S SECRET CHILDREN

**Six siblings discover they're actually part of
the notorious Fortune family and move to
Chatelaine, Texas, to claim their name...while
uncovering shocking truths and life-changing
surprises. Will their Fortunes turn—hopefully,
for the better?**

At a convention in Las Vegas, rancher
Dahlia Fortune's none too pleased to encounter
her childhood rival and new next door neighbor,
Rawlston Ames. But after an unexpectedly giddy
reunion becomes more, they awaken the next
day—to discover they're husband and wife! Much
to Dahlia's surprise, though, this mishap of a
marriage might not be such a mistake after all...

Dear Reader,

I finally got to write a cowgirl heroine! This is my first honest-to-goodness Western rancher romance. And they're *both* ranchers! And yes—I am excited. I grew up dreaming of horses and cowboys. In my teens, I got my first horse, and spent years riding, showing, training and raising them.

So when Harlequin asked me to write another *Fortunes of Texas* book, I was thrilled when I discovered the heroine, Dahlia, is a horse lover, lives on the family ranch and raises sheep. And the guy she wakes up married to in Las Vegas? Well, Rawlston Ames is the cattle rancher next door. They share a fence line *and* the huge secret of their impulsive Vegas wedding (spiked punch may have been involved). Dahlia's in a hurry to end the sham wedding, but Rawlston keeps coming up with excuses not to sign those annulment papers she keeps waving in his face.

I want to thank my El Paso in-laws for hosting us and helping me understand Texas, and my brother and sister-in-law for joining me on a giant Texas adventure last fall—from Houston to Dallas. I'd like to thank editor Susan Litman and my agent, Jill Marsal. And I'd like to thank my very own cowboy, Himself. He never lets me forget that he won a blue ribbon at his first horse show, while I came in second! I was, and am, so proud of him. He's my biggest cheerleader, and my very own Happily Ever After.

Jo McNally

FORTUNE'S SECRET MARRIAGE

JO McNALLY

Harlequin

THE FORTUNES OF TEXAS

Special thanks and acknowledgment are given to
Jo McNally for her contribution to
The Fortunes of Texas: Fortune's Secret Children miniseries.

 Harlequin®
THE FORTUNES
OF TEXAS

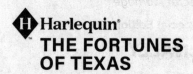

Recycling programs
for this product may
not exist in your area.

ISBN-13: 978-1-335-99672-5

Fortune's Secret Marriage

Copyright © 2024 by Harlequin Enterprises ULC

Harlequin Enterprises ULC
22 Adelaide St. West, 41st Floor
Toronto, Ontario M5H 4E3, Canada
www.Harlequin.com

Printed in Lithuania

MIX
Paper | Supporting
responsible forestry
FSC® C021394

Award-winning romance author **Jo McNally** lives in her beloved upstate New York with her very own romance hero husband. When she's not writing or reading romance novels, she loves to travel and explore new places and experiences. She's a big fan of leisurely lunches with her besties. Her favorite room at home is the sunroom, where she enjoys both morning coffee and evening cocktails with her husband while listening to an eclectic (and often Irish) playlist.

Books by Jo McNally

The Fortunes of Texas: Fortune's Secret Children

Fortune's Secret Marriage

Harlequin Special Edition

Winsome Cove

A Cape Cod Summer

Gallant Lake Stories

A Man You Can Trust
It Started at Christmas...
Her Homecoming Wish
Changing His Plans
Her Mountainside Haven
Second-Chance Summer
Expecting His Holiday Surprise

The Fortunes of Texas: The Wedding Gift

A Soldier's Dare

Harlequin Superromance

Nora's Guy Next Door
She's Far From Hollywood

Visit the Author Profile page
at Harlequin.com for more titles.

This book is dedicated to my lovely Texas cousin-in-law (and avid reader!), Judy.

Chapter One

Dahlia Fortune's Western boots clicked on the marble floor like stilettos as she strode across the lobby of the Indigo Blaze Casino and Convention Center. Heads began to turn, and she slowed her pace. She didn't usually move quite so…aggressively…but her dislike of Las Vegas was showing.

She was a Texas cowgirl through and through. She liked open vistas and the smell of saddle leather and horses. And just because she was staying in a luxurious suite at the hotel this week, she really wasn't one for the trappings of the rich and famous. She supposed she *was* wealthy, but thankfully *not* famous. Crowds weren't her thing, and she definitely didn't want to be the center of attention.

She could handle it when needed, of course. After all, she was the daughter of a ruthless businessman—who was *not* a Fortune—and he'd raised her and her five siblings to be ready to take on the world without showing any sign of weakness. That didn't mean she *liked* it. Dahlia would rather be riding a horse or sitting alone working on her needle felt art. But the national sheep farmers convention was winding to a close, and she didn't want to miss the Best in Show competition coming up.

Her pace slowed again as she found herself stuck behind yet *another* wedding party. She'd been bumping into brides and grooms all week—yet another reason to dislike Vegas. There were weddings happening *everywhere*. Elvis weddings, superhero weddings, grunge weddings, champagne weddings… The only thing they *usually* had in common was one or both wearing some sort of wedding veil. The gift shops were full of the things, in every color, length and price point.

The couple in front of her now had brought friends, and the whole crowd had clearly been partying for a while. They were carrying champagne bottles, waving them in the air as the hotel staff watched warily to make sure the bottles weren't open. The two grooms each wore white tuxedo jackets over… Speedos. Their veils matched the swim trunks—one orange and one green. She guessed they were Irish, and it was confirmed when one of their pals started step-dancing.

Vegas weddings were ridiculous. But she'd yet to see a newly hitched duo who didn't look ecstatically happy and in love. Well…a few of them were too drunk to be sure about the *in love* part. Those couples got sloppier as the nights grew later, sometimes barely holding each other up. But they seemed happy. And they were, well… married. Something *she* hadn't managed to accomplish in her thirty-two years on this planet.

Dahlia managed to work her way past the Irish wedding and turned down the hallway leading to the exhibition arena. She was hoping that whole *unmarried* issue would be resolved as soon as her boyfriend, Carter Powers, returned from his business trip to Europe. It seemed like she was always waiting on Carter to show up lately, with all his business travel and now, talk of running for office. He'd been a little distant emotionally, too, after her move from Cactus Grove to Chatelaine and changing her last name from Windham to Fortune.

Carter wasn't big on being *impulsive*, and she'd been nothing *but* that over the past few months—ever since her father's death and Mom's stunning discovery about her past. Turns out Wendy Fortune was a long-lost member of the well-known Fortune family, meaning her children were Fortunes, too. Dahlia and her siblings had all been dealing with so many changes in their lives at the time, so why not honor Mom's request that they take the Fortune name and move to Chatelaine to be closer to other members of the Fortune family? Although, admittedly, some did so with more enthusiasm than others.

Dad had been...difficult. Hard. Cold. Demanding. Still, a name change was a big step. But he was gone and their mother was here. And when sweet Wendy Wind— er, make that Wendy *Fortune*—wanted something, she had a way of making it happen. In this case, she'd done so by buying a massive working ranch on Lake Chatelaine with six luxury lakefront log homes on it. One for each of her children.

Dahlia couldn't blame Carter for being overwhelmed with her life choices in the six months since they'd met. But she still had a hunch he was coming back from Europe with an engagement ring. He was always talking of what a great match they made. In fact, he said that more than he mentioned how much he loved her. He tended to talk about loving *them* together more than loving *her*.

But despite her father's personal faults, she respected Carter for being a hard-driving businessman like her dad had been. If he was approaching marriage from a practical point of view, she had no problem with that. It *was* a merger of sorts. It wasn't like *she* was all emotional about things, either. She cared for Carter. And as far as she was concerned, that was a solid foundation for marriage.

Some people got too caught up in the mushy romance stuff instead of focusing on compatibility. Her parents had lived largely separate lives, but they'd made their partnership work...for the most part. Dahlia entered the exhibition center, smiling at her naked left hand as she pushed the door open. Soon she'd be sporting a diamond—she was sure of it.

The Best in Show competition was just starting, and she hurried to the main arena. The Dorper sheep were so cute, with their black faces and floppy ears. They looked like the *Shaun the Sheep* character in the popular animated TV show. But *cute* wasn't a factor in her decision-making this week. Instead, she searched for Sally Mathison and her award-winning Texas Merino sheep. It was no surprise to find the older woman in the arena with a beautiful, fluffy ram with short, curly horns. The ram had already won Best of Breed and, just as Dahlia walked up to the fence, Yellow Ross of Texas won Best in Show.

Dahlia applauded with the other sheep farmers watching, satisfied that she'd made the right decision. Ross would be moving to the Fortune Family Ranch next week, along with thirty ewes. Another fifty sheep would arrive from two other farms farther north, in Texas Hill

Country. They would be the beginning of Dahlia's dream coming true—raising her own sheep and selling their highly prized merino wool. And, of course, she'd use the wool for her own crafts, too. She caught Sally's eye and gave her a thumbs-up across the ring. Tomorrow, she'd head home to Texas and inform her family that she'd be adding sheep to the ranch livestock.

Across the sheep pens, she saw a tall man with a vaguely familiar stride moving through the crowd. He wore a well-worn cowboy hat and a dark blue Western shirt. She froze.

No. It couldn't be…

At that moment, he looked up as if she'd called out to him. His gray-eyed gaze slammed into hers from forty feet away. It was him. Rawlston Ames. *Damn it*. The guy had been her nemesis since grade school, floating through life with his *aw-shucks* charm and deep Texas drawl. Always outdoing her in school and in most of the livestock shows. She'd work herself to exhaustion and he'd stroll into the ring and flash that killer smile at the judges, then waltz out with the blue ribbon.

To be fair, the guy was legitimately smart and his family had a successful ranch in Cactus Grove. He'd been an only child with adoring parents. So yes, she might have been just a bit jealous. Rawlston had such a knack for showing up at the most annoying times, though. It wasn't until after she'd agreed to move to Chatelaine with her family that she discovered Rawlston owned a large ranch there. One that bordered the Fortune Family Ranch. Just her luck.

And now, here he was in Vegas. At a *sheep* show. She turned on her heel. Maybe he hadn't recognized her.

"Dahlia! Wait up!"

She kept walking, hoping she was just imagining that was Rawlston's voice. She was having a good day, and if that guy had suddenly decided to be a sheep farmer, too, she'd absolutely lose it.

"Dahlia! Wait!"

He was closer now, and she stopped. Running from him would be undignified. He was almost at her side by the time she turned. She couldn't help noticing the random women watching him with interest. Yeah, he was that kind of guy. Tall and lanky, with a stride as smooth as his voice. A man's man who made the ladies swoon. So *irritating*. She put her hands on her hips.

"What the hell are you doing here?"

Rawlston chuckled in surprise. Leave it to Dahlia Windham Fortune to waste no time in setting him back on his heels. She'd been doing it since high school.

"I think what you *meant* to say is 'Hi, Rawlston, how nice to see you again.'"

Color rose on her porcelain cheeks. "That's the thing, though," she answered. "I keep seeing you everywhere lately. Even after I moved to Chatelaine—surprise— *you* now live in Chatelaine. I decide to raise sheep, and suddenly you're here at the sheepherding convention in Las Vegas. I thought you raised cattle?"

"I do, and I'm not planning on changing livestock anytime soon." Rawlston nodded off to his right. "I was in town for a farm equipment convention and stopped by to say hi to a navy pal who's a vendor here for animal husbandry supplies." He reached out and touched her shoulder, moving the two of them out of the way of a teen boy pulling a cart loaded with hay bales and bags of feed. Exhibitors were packing up now that the show was over. "Are you really looking to raise sheep?"

Some of her brittleness eased, and her chin rose in pride. "The Best in Show ram will be moving to Chatelaine next week."

"Congratulations. I didn't know the Fortune Family Ranch was branching into the sheep biz."

She gave a flippant one-shoulder shrug. "They don't all know about it yet. But it's a big ranch. I'm sure they can handle me raising a few sheep on my portion."

Rawlston wasn't so sure about that. The Windhams... he caught himself. He knew they were Fortunes now, but he'd known them as Windhams his entire life. Whatever their names were now, they could be a prickly bunch. Their dad, Casper Windham, had been a real SOB. Arrogant, greedy, detached. His one love was Windham Plastics, a mega producer of plastic products that had been the target of environmentalists for years. Casper had seemed to regard his six children as assets more than family.

That kind of upbringing affected a kid. Rawlston had gone to school with Dahlia and her siblings, and each of them seemed to absorb the stress of their cold, demanding father differently. But they'd all come through it intact, as far as he could see. They'd each developed their own defense mechanisms, from being driven and competitive to overpleasing. Dahlia fell closer to the driven end of the spectrum. She'd always been fiercely independent.

An older woman walked up to them, giving Dahlia

a quick hug. The woman was obviously a rancher, with her trim jeans and well-worn boots and hat.

"How about that Ross, huh?" the woman said, beaming. "You bought yourself a champion!" She turned to Rawlston. "Sorry to interrupt you two. I'm Sally Mathison, owner of the Mathison Ranch outside of Dallas. And you must be the boyfriend—"

"No!" Dahlia almost shouted the denial, making Rawlston smile. He'd rarely seen her get flustered. "This is *not* Carter. This is…" She glanced at him, then away again. "This is just someone I used to know in high school." *Ouch.* "He has a ranch near mine in Chatelaine. We're neighbors, I think…"

She was starting to babble, so he held out his hand to Sally. "Rawlston Ames. My ranch borders the Fortune ranch. I stopped to say hi to a friend and ran into Dahlia."

"Well, if you're a neighbor you're still invited."

"Invited to what?"

"There's an exhibitor's reception near the pool to celebrate the end of the show. Dahlia is officially a sheep rancher now, and her ram just won Best in Show, so the two of you should join us."

"Oh…" Dahlia stammered. "I… I appreciate it, but—"

"We'll be there," Rawlston said.

"Great! See you both there!"

Sally hurried off, and Dahlia was staring at him in fury.

"What?" He splayed his hands wide in innocence. "If you're gonna raise sheep, you need to build relationships with people in the business. A casual reception like this is a great opportunity for you."

"If there's one thing I don't need, it's some man making decisions for me. And what do *you* get out of it? I have a boyfriend, you know. A *serious* one. Carter Powers."

Rawlston did his best not to let his disgust show. Carter was a world-class jackass. The dude thought he was some brilliant businessman, but most of his success had come from riding other people's coattails, stealing other people's ideas and bamboozling his clients. One of those former clients was Rawlston's dad. He had no idea why Dahlia was with the guy, but her taste in dating had always baffled him.

Truth be told, Rawlston had had a mad crush on her in high school, but she'd always gone for the nerds or the superrich boys. The kind of boys her father would approve of. She'd never given a jock like him a second glance. Stung at her rejection, he'd dated casually, earning a reputation as a ladies' man. It was what was expected from the high school quarterback, but he'd never been serious about anyone. However, he'd always known when tall, elegant Dahlia entered a room. She'd walked down the halls like she owned the place, and students would make way for her as if she was royalty.

"Free food and drink?" He finally answered her question, pushing aside thoughts of his childhood crush on her. No good could come from those memories. Besides, if she was the type of woman who dated a guy like Carter, she wasn't the woman for him. "Look, I was already going. My pal Mike invited me. So we can walk there together or separately. Your choice. And for the record…yes, I know you have a boyfriend."

Dahlia studied him for a moment, then relaxed. Had

she really thought he'd been hitting on her? "Fine," she relented. "There's nothing wrong with two neighbors walking to a reception together."

Two neighbors. Not even *two friends*. He watched her walk away, her blond hair swinging in time with her hips. Still tall and slender, wearing simple chinos and a denim jacket, Dahlia had somehow picked up even *more* elegance through the years. But old, unrequited feelings aside, there was no escaping the fact that the two of them had always been lifelong competitors, in everything from grades—she was valedictorian, he was salutatorian—to livestock competitions.

She could outride him in the horse ring, but he had the prize cattle every year. He smiled to himself. One year she'd decided to raise piglets, so he'd convinced his parents to let him do the same. His litter won at the county fair.

Rawlston stopped. No wonder she hadn't been thrilled to see him. He'd been kind of a jerk to her back then. It was high school stuff, but still. Maybe he'd deserved her anger. Dahlia glanced over her shoulder, and he hustled to catch up with her.

They were neighbors, after all. Tonight he'd show her he knew how to be a *good* neighbor. Maybe even a friend. Nothing more than that…no matter how tempting.

Chapter Two

When did Rawlston Ames become so fascinating?

Dahlia took another sip of her fruit punch and stared into his mesmerizing gray-blue eyes, trying to pay attention to the story he was telling about buying his prize bull. Those eyes were really something. And his deep voice and slow drawl…

She sat up straight and gave herself a mental scolding. Rawlston had *never* been her type, and he wasn't going to start now. She was just tired. It had been a while since she'd relaxed and just let herself have a good time. For whatever reason, that was what had happened tonight.

She and Rawlston were in a booth near the appetizer table at the poolside exhibitor's reception, although the actual reception had wound down an hour ago. Most of the food had been cleared, other than a cheese and cracker tray and the bowl of virgin fruit punch sitting at the end of the table.

They'd headed in separate directions when they'd first arrived. Rawlston went to chat with his navy buddy near the bar, and Dahlia had followed his advice and networked her way around the room. She'd talked with sheep ranchers from all over the West, and some who had traveled from as far as Canada. She might be new at this business, but she wanted to show she was serious and that she'd done her homework.

As the evening wore on, she'd found herself with a group of women who'd glommed onto a group of guys, which included Rawlston and his buddy Mike. Dahlia wasn't there to hook up with anyone, so when Rawlston gave her a tip of his head as if to say *let's leave these young'uns* she'd followed him to the far side of the pool. The table near the food was her choice—she needed something to absorb the chardonnay she'd been drinking all evening, and the fruit punch was mighty refreshing.

They'd talked about relocating to Chatelaine, and Rawlston told her where the farm supply and feedstore was and which businesses to check out, like the upscale LC Club. Apparently the town was often a comparison of opposites—dusty ranches amid the mansions of the wealthy. He told her about his herd of prize beef cattle at his Chatelaine ranch. Of course, he just had to mention the *prize* part—competitive as ever. Then he shared how he and his dad had come to Chatelaine for a fresh start after Rawlston's mother had died of cancer back in Cactus Grove.

Rawlston refilled their punch glasses whenever they were empty, and the conversation rolled along so easily that she began wondering if she'd misjudged the man. He was witty and charming, with an easy smile and such great stories. *So many* stories, and they were great. All of them. Really great.

Dahlia had shared some stories, too. She was actually surprised how talkative she'd become. She wasn't usually this chatty unless she'd been drinking. She told him about the discovery of her mother's past—that Wendy was a secret baby from long ago, and the woman who'd raised her wasn't her mother at all. The woman was a babysitter who'd raised Wendy as her own after her parents died in the tragic mine collapse that was such a big part of Chatelaine's history.

The mine collapse had killed fifty men. There were signs all around Chatelaine saying *Remember the 50*. There was even a small museum dedicated to the incident. History-loving tourists came to Chatelaine to learn more about the mining disaster. But it turned out there were actually fifty-*one* people who had perished. The fifty-first was a woman—Wendy's young mother, Ariella, who'd rushed to the mine to tell the father of her child something urgent. Their relationship, and the baby, had been a secret, because Ariella's father, Wendell Fortune, had forbidden them from seeing each other. The baby—Dahlia's mother—became an orphan that day.

Wendy had never known, until this year, that she'd been the secret illegitimate granddaughter and heir of the recently deceased Wendell Fortune. That discovery came on the heels of the death of Casper Windham, and everyone's tangled feelings about Casper made them more receptive to move as a family to Chatelaine for a fresh start, just like Rawlston and his father had done.

So…they had *that* in common. Which was funny, right? It must have been funny, because they were both laughing so hard about it right now. Or…laughing about something. Who cared what? It felt good to laugh again, and Dahlia put her hand on Rawlston's arm and leaned closer. Which wasn't hard to do because they were now sitting side by side in the booth. He'd joined her on her side of the table after refilling their punch glasses again. Such a clever guy. Why had she ever disliked this man? She couldn't remember. *Damn, this punch is delicious.*

Rawlston took her hand and wound his fingers into hers. That was nice. Wait…she wasn't supposed to be feeling nice with another man. She was engaged, well, almost. She snort-laughed at herself. Almost didn't count, right?

"This isn't horseshoes." She hadn't intended to say that out loud, and the sound of the words in her oddly elevated voice made her giggle. Rawlston grinned. He had a fantastic grin, especially when he let it show in his eyes, which were twinkling right now.

"Uh, no," he said. "This is definitely not horseshoes. Would you like it to be?" He scooted closer to her, putting her back to the wall. "Do you want to get points for being close?"

There was a dim voice in the back of her mind warning that this was a really bad, possibly disastrous, idea. Rawlston leaned in, his shirt brushing her chest. His hand touched the corner of her mouth lightly. Was the room spinning, or was that just her?

He held up his thumb, where he'd wiped a drop of punch from her chin.

"You're wasting perfectly good punch, Dahlia."

She licked it from his thumb and felt a shocking jolt of white-hot desire sweep through her. Rawlston felt it, too—his eyes went from gray to cobalt in an instant.

Bad idea! Horrible idea! Abort! Abort!

She straightened, breaking the moment. He sat back enough to give her some space and a chance to shake off whatever had just happened between them.

"Whew, is it getting hotter tonight or what?" She fanned herself with her hand, then reached for her glass and drained it. "If it wasn't for this punch I'd be melted into a puddle. Speaking of which…?" She held up her empty glass. Rawlston took it with a smile.

"I don't think it's the heat that's melting you, Dolly. But it's probably time to call it a night." Ever the practical cowboy, doing the right thing, even when neither of them wanted tonight to end. He took their glasses. "But this *is* damn good punch. One more to clear our heads, okay?" He slid out of the booth to get refills. He was just sitting back down when there was a commotion behind him.

"Spencer!" A woman's voice was nearly shrieking. "What in the blue blazes are you *doing*? Oh my gawd…"

The woman, with a teased bubble of white-blond hair and a sparkly gold jacket over a white leather miniskirt, was confronting a young teen boy. They were having a heated discussion while Rawlston and Dahlia toasted each other with their punch glasses.

"Here's to a new friendship between former rivals." Dahlia wondered why her voice was all soft and sultry. Sure, they'd had lots of sparks in this booth tonight, but it didn't mean anything. It wasn't real. Just two acquaintances innocently finding a friendly connection. Even if she *did* want to see how that firm mouth felt on her skin. She flushed and downed her punch in one gulp. *This isn't real.*

Rawlston chuckled. "Here's to hot nights, cool punch and beautiful women." His eyes never left hers as he drained his glass. Why was she thinking she wanted him to swallow *her* like that—like a man starved for a woman?

Another mental reprimand—*Stop it*. Rawlston Ames was gorgeous and rich. He could have any woman he wanted, and he'd never once wanted her. Not in high school. Not in college. Not now. A sudden wave of melancholy washed over her. For some reason her emotions were all ramped up tonight.

"Hey…" His voice, smooth as butter and warm as whiskey, broke through her thoughts. "Why the frown?" His fingers touched her chin and lifted it. "I like happy Dolly better."

She'd never liked that nickname, and he kept using it. She should be mad, but instead, it felt intimate and nostalgic. She blinked back the moisture in her eyes. Was she *crying*? Something was definitely off with her. Rawlston was right, it was time to get back to her room and get some sleep.

They left the booth and made one last stop at the punch bowl, both giggling as they grabbed nearby water glasses and filled them to the top "to go." As they were leaving the table, the bubble-haired lady in gold sequins stopped them. She was weaving, and her eyes seemed a bit unfocused. Or was that Dahlia who was weaving?

"Is that the punch from the poolside table?" The woman was almost whispering, which did nothing to dim her thick Southern accent. "I'm pretty sure my knucklehead nephew poured vodka into that bowl. Like…a *lot* of vodka. He took a full bottle from our room. Actually, it might be more than one." She closed her eyes with a dramatic sigh. "I was just headed to tell the hotel staff that I saw a mouse in the punch or something so they'll throw it out. I mean, Spencer's an idiot, but he's only fourteen, and I don't want him in trouble. Besides, we were supposed to be watching him while my sister and her husband go to her husband's brother's wedding, which is one of those Elvis circus weddings that will never last."

Dahlia and Rawlston looked at each other and each raised a brow. This woman's story was endless.

"My point is, I can't in good conscience let you drink too much of that punch without knowing the truth. Consider yourselves warned."

She dashed away, leaving the two of them staring from each other to their glasses. They'd already been drinking that punch for two hours. *Weird.*

Rawlston spoke first. "That lady's crazy. If this punch was spiked with that much vodka, you and I would be on the floor by now." As if to prove his point, he gulped down the punch in his glass, then gave her an exaggerated, lip-smacking sigh of satisfaction.

Dahlia nodded in agreement. "I was thinking the same thing. That kid sure has her fooled." She took another healthy sip from her glass. "He probably drank the booze himself." Then she drained the rest of it. *See?* She felt totally fine.

Rawlston took her arm and leaned in. *Damn this man smells good.* "Probably. But just to be safe, let's see if I can walk you to your room without us accidentally falling into some Vegas wedding chapel."

Dahlia clutched his arm—his thick, hard, warm bicep—and laughed. Was her laughter suddenly extra loud?

Must be the empty hallway.

"As tempting as being married by Elvis would be, I think I'll be able to avoid buying a hot pink wedding veil and saying *I do* to you, Rawlston Ames."

* * *

Rawlston woke up with a pounding headache. Even worse, there was a blazing bright light shining on his face. He raised his arm to shield his eyes. *What the hell is that?* He winced and blinked a few times before he realized it was the sun. Looking around his suite at the Indigo Blaze Casino, he saw it was daytime, and well into it judging from the height of the sun in the sky. He'd clearly forgotten to close the drapes before going to bed last night. Oddly enough, he didn't remember getting back to his suite or getting undressed. But he definitely felt naked under the sheets right now.

He glanced down to confirm and his whole world came skidding to a halt. Including his heart.

It wasn't a blanket keeping him warm.

It was a *woman*, sprawled across him like a starfish. She was lying face down, her head turned away from him.

Rawlston touched her arm and she made a soft sound and shifted slightly. Okay, she was breathing, so this wasn't an episode of *Law & Order: SVU*. But who the hell *was* she? He scrubbed his hand down his face and tried to remember what happened after he walked Dahlia to her room last night.

He must have gone back down to the bar, because he and Dahlia had been drinking punch while they'd talked for hours. Furrowing his brow, he winced as his head pain increased right between his eyes. Sure, that weird lady had told them the punch was spiked, but they'd both dismissed it. They hadn't been drunk. Another throb of pain. Or *had* they?

Nah. He must have gone drinking after and picked

up some woman at a club. Not his finest moment, but not the end of the world, either.

He shifted gently to sit up, eliciting another groan from his bedmate. To his relief, there was a used condom on the floor. Even in a drunken romp, he'd used protection. The woman's left hand moved to the top of the sheet. She was wearing a wedding band.

He muttered a curse. It was one thing to have a random one-night stand in Las Vegas. But he wasn't the kind of guy to bring a *married* woman to his room, no matter how drunk he'd been. Maybe his drink had been drugged? He looked around the room. No, he hadn't been robbed. He could see his wallet, phone and laptop. Besides, she wouldn't spike her own drink, and she was still passed out. He reached out to touch her hand, and had another shock.

He was wearing a wedding band. And it matched the one on *her* hand. They were both platinum, with a center stripe of textured gold. He yanked his off like it was burning him. It was inscribed inside—*RA and DF Forever.*

He glanced at the long blond hair sweeping across the sheets. *No. It couldn't be.* He touched the woman's hair and she made an annoyed sound and turned her face toward him, eyes still closed in slumber.

Dahlia Fortune.

He blinked a few times, as if that was going to change what he was seeing. *Dahlia* was naked in his bed. They were wearing matching wedding bands, and she was wearing a sparkling diamond engagement ring. There was a long bridal veil draped over the desk chair in his room. Some fake pink roses, edges gilded with gold glitter, were scattered on the floor. They were in Las

Vegas. It didn't take much of a leap to realize what had happened. But *why*? And...*how*?

For some reason, he slid the ring back onto his finger. In between head throbs, he was starting to piece together snippets of memory from last night. Laughing at all the bridal couples. Seeing the gift shop... No, they went *into* the gift shop. Dahlia was trying on veils and chortling something about wanting his opinion on what color she could get. Then she'd found one that not only sparkled, but *lit up* with tiny LED lights. They'd been acting silly—uncharacteristic for either of them.

He remembered being surprised that the shop actually had a small selection of high-end rings, including diamonds. Another couple rushed in, breathlessly grabbing a hot pink veil and a matching bow tie the groom put on above his grunge rock T-shirt. When they'd left, Rawlston couldn't remember if it was Dahlia or him who had said something like, *If you can't beat them, join them.* The words were a dare neither would back down from. He did now recall a pink chapel. A female officiate wearing pink tulle. An elevator ride that was a blur of kisses. And judging from the rumpled look of the bed, they'd had one hell of a night.

As a *married* couple.

He closed his eyes tightly, shaking his head. What had they been thinking? How many bottles of vodka had that kid poured into the fruit punch? This was going to be a mess of epic proportions. But Rawlston was a problem solver at heart, and there had to be a solution to this one. Surely these things happened a lot in Vegas, and could be quietly annulled. First, he needed to wake

Dahlia and see how much she remembered about their very busy night. His hand hesitated above her shoulder.

He had a hunch she was *not* going to be thrilled to wake up as Mrs. Rawlston Ames.

Chapter Three

Dahlia heard her name being spoken, but she did *not* want to wake up. She was warm and comfortable and her body felt heavy from physical exertion. She muttered, "Go away," and turned her head. A hand touched her shoulder.

A *hand* touched her shoulder. There shouldn't be any damn hands in her hotel suite.

She jolted awake, shocked to find she was sharing a bed with someone. Not just someone…a *male* someone. And he was touching her. And she was *naked*. She catapulted out of bed with a scream, twisting the sheet around herself like a toga.

"Where am I? Why am I naked? Did you *drug* me? Oh my God. Where's my phone? Where's my stuff?" Panic choked her words, and all she could think was that the worst had happened.

The man moved and Dahlia shouted at him. "Don't you move! I don't know what happened last night, but I'm calling the…"

"Dahlia." The voice was firm and steady. And familiar. For the first time, she dared to look at his face.

"Rawlston?"

Confusion replaced her panic. She couldn't imagine him doing anything to purposefully harm her. And yet…they'd been naked in bed together. And she had no memory of coming to his suite. She sat on the far corner of the large bed, her legs no longer willing to support her. She clutched the sheet around her body.

"I don't understand…" She felt foolish for admitting that, but she needed answers. His response was to hold up his left hand and waggle his fingers. He had a wedding band on. She rolled her eyes. "Yes, I know you were married. But isn't it time to take that thing off?" She'd heard he and Lana divorced a few years ago.

He seemed shockingly unperturbed by this…this *situation*. In fact, he looked downright amused. What was she missing? He nodded toward her hand. She looked down and inhaled sharply.

She was also wearing a wedding band. And it matched the one on Rawlston's hand. Above it was a diamond solitaire.

"No-o-o-o-o…" The protest came out as a moan of disbelief. This wasn't possible.

"I hate to argue on our honeymoon, but…apparently yes." A corner of the comforter was covering his private parts, but there was a whole lot of Rawlston Ames on display. Some remote corner of her mind noted, even in crisis, that he was a fine specimen of a man. Lean and hard and tanned. *Wait.* Did he just say *honeymoon*?

"We cannot be married. It makes no sense. I don't even remember." She narrowed her eyes at him. Maybe he wasn't as trustworthy as she'd thought. "Why can't I remember?"

Rawlston gave her an understanding smile. "It took a bit for it to come back to me, too. Do you remember that lady who claimed her nephew spiked the punch we'd been drinking for hours?"

Dahlia's head was throbbing and fuzzy, but she did recall the woman in leather and sequins. She nodded and Rawlston continued.

"We were so sure she was wrong, but now I can see that was the vodka talking. Think about it—we were talking nonstop for hours, and laughing up a storm. You and me. We're far from friends." He glanced at the bed. "Well, we're *more* than friends now, I guess, but you know what I mean. It was out of character—booze-fueled—and it didn't end when we left the reception."

She closed her eyes tightly, willing this to all go away. But as bits and pieces of the evening came into focus, she realized he was right. They'd been laughing and giggling like little kids. She'd been fingering his biceps and getting lost in his eyes. Then more things came to mind. The gift shop. The jewelry counter. A laughing dare…

"Does pink tulle spark any memories?" he asked softly.

Her eyes snapped open.

"The chapel," she breathed. "Everything was covered in pink tulle. I had a veil…"

He pointed to the chair, where a long white veil was draped. "It lights up."

A horrified laugh bubbled up. Was it possible that she'd gotten drunk and had a Barbie wedding in a battery-operated veil? That Rawlston Ames was actually her *husband*? She put her hand down on the bed to support herself, suddenly dizzy. She was *married* to one of the most annoying men she'd ever met. Her fingers tightened on the sheet. And they'd clearly had quite a night together in this bed. Her body was aching, but in the nicest way. She straightened at one more horrifying thought.

Carter. She tried not to question why it took this much time for her boyfriend's existence to enter her mind. But they *were* dating, and he'd been hinting at a future together. How the hell was she going to tell him she was *married*? And why had she and Carter never left a bed looking this disheveled or her body feeling this sated in their six months together? *No, that isn't important right now.*

"I can't be married to you. I have a boyfriend, Rawlston."

"Cheating on your husband already, eh?" His smug grin infuriated her.

"This is *Not. Funny.* This is my *life* we're talking about, and none of my life plans included marrying *you*."

"And yet, here we are." He raised his hand when she started to argue. "I get it—it wasn't on my bingo card, either. But the fact is, you and I did get married last night, and we can't turn back the clock to change our lousy decision-making, so getting hysterical won't help."

Dahlia went still. "Did you just tell a woman not to get hysterical?" Uncertainty clouded his eyes as she continued. "It is *not* hysterical to be concerned about telling the man I'm dating that *oops*, I accidentally married someone else. That is a genuine and legitimate problem for me, Rawlston. And my family…"

As if her mother and siblings hadn't dealt with enough this year, now she was going to add a scandalous Vegas wedding to the mix. Instead of wooing the future governor of Texas, she'd be letting them down by marrying some rancher. Of course, *they* were technically all ranchers, now, but still. She'd been a constant disappointment to them over the years. Or at least, to her father. He'd never missed a chance to tell her she was "wasting herself" by being a lowly horse groomer or worse, wanting to raise sheep. She'd started dating Carter just before her father's death, and Casper Windham had been thrilled that she was linking two prominent Dallas-area families together.

For the first time, Rawlston lost his aura of calm acceptance. He was scowling now, his jaw working back and forth.

"Okay. Yeah, you're right. I didn't mean to diminish the seriousness of what we've done. But every problem has a solution, and we'll figure this out." His gaze slid down her body and she felt an odd tingle on her skin. He looked away with a sigh, staring out the window. "I think we'll tackle it more maturely with clothes on, don't you? Why don't you use the shower first, and I'll order us some breakfast. Brains work better on a full stomach."

Every problem has a solution.

Brains work better on a full stomach.

He was always so full of practical platitudes. His calmness could be grating, but he was right. Breakfast, a shower, and clothing sounded like a good idea. But there was one thing she didn't need to wait to make a decision on. She stood, holding the sheet in front of her with one hand and pointing at him with the other.

"We can't tell *anyone* about this, Rawlston. Not a soul. I will *not* go back to Chatelaine as Mrs. Rawlston Ames." The thought gave her a chill. "These things must happen all the time in this town, so there has to be a way to annul it quickly and easily. No one else needs to know."

He stared at her for a moment, studying her face intently. "I'm not sure how quick and easy it will be, and it sure won't happen before we go home tonight. So technically, you *will* go back to Texas as Mrs. Rawlston Ames." He cut her off before she could object. "But I promise not to call you that there. It'll be our little secret."

There was nothing *little* about this mess, but she was satisfied with his answer. She turned toward the bathroom and stopped by the dresser. Their marriage certificate was sitting on top. She groaned and slid the rings off her finger, leaving them on the pink piece of paper and giving him a pointed look.

"One thing you can do before we leave is return these rings."

There was a pause, then he called out as she walked into the bathroom. "Does that mean no conjugal visits once we're in Chatelaine, Mrs. Ames? It looks like we had fun... *Ow!*"

He ducked from the box of tissues she'd thrown at his head, and it bounced off his shoulder.

"That is your one and only time to call me that. Whatever happened last night will *never* happen again. Return those rings."

"Yes, ma'am!" He was cackling when she slammed the bathroom door closed. *Jackass.*

She was trying to suppress any bits of memory from their night in his bed, but she knew her body was going to be remembering his touch long after they were no longer married.

Rawlston stepped out onto his back porch with a mug of coffee in one hand and a rawhide bone in the other.

Tripp, his Australian cattle dog, was right at his heel, watching him intently. Correction—watching the *bone* intently. After a few feints, Rawlston tossed the bone far into the yard and the black and white dog tore after it. That would give him a few minutes to himself before Tripp demanded more attention. Tripp had spent four days with Rawlston's dad while Rawlston was in Vegas. He'd no doubt been sleeping on the furniture and being fed hand-cooked slices of chicken and beef. That fool dog had had more of a vacation than Rawlston, but Tripp was still playing the victim now that they were home.

Smiling despite himself, Rawlston walked across the patio and stared out over the range behind the low-slung barns. The sun was just peeking over the horizon. The main cattle herd was nowhere in sight, but that wasn't unusual on a fifteen-hundred-acre ranch. They were probably out by the creek that ran near the border of his ranch and the Fortune ranch. In a smaller pasture near the barns, a few cows and calves were grazing.

Instead of the more common Herefords, he raised Brahmans. Originally from Africa, Brahman cattle had distinctive humps above their shoulders, and the males were often used in rodeos for bull riding. But they were good beef producers, and tolerated the Texas heat well.

Rawlston's red brick house was long and low like the barns, but at least twice as old. He'd bought this place for the land, not the amenities. It was just a house—nothing fancy. It kept him cool and dry and held the comfortable, overstuffed furniture that he liked. He'd furnished all three bedrooms but two of them had rarely been slept in. A few high school or navy pals and his dad were the only people who occasionally stayed over if the talking or drinking ran late. When he bought the ranch a few years ago, the real estate agent had assumed he'd use this house for staff housing and would build something more impressive for himself. But he wasn't into impressing people. The dog let out a bark, standing on alert as he watched a jackrabbit tear across the back of the yard.

"Stand down, dog." Three-year-old Tripp was a well-trained herding and hunting machine, and he knew when he had permission to run and when he didn't. He quivered until the rabbit was out of sight, then heaved a sigh and came back up into the shade. It was going to be yet another hundred-degree early August day.

Tripp might have been spoiled staying with Rawlston's dad, but he still hadn't had as exciting a weekend as Rawlston had. He'd come home from Vegas a married man. Albeit temporarily. He'd agreed with Dahlia's demand that he remove the wedding band, but he hadn't returned the rings. They were all together in a small box tucked into his sock drawer.

He sat on the bench and watched the sun rising higher in a clear sky. Hoping it would give him clarity. Because in all honesty, he wasn't sure why he'd kept the rings. Dahlia was right—they needed to end this sham marriage right away. He had zero interest in ever being married again to anyone, and she'd made it clear that she felt the same about *him*. Rawlston scowled into his coffee mug. She wanted that sleazeball Carter Powers. Carter was another reminder that Dahlia wasn't the kind of woman he'd ever be compatible with. Sure, he'd always admired her cool confidence back in school, and basked in her beauty as she grew into her willowy body and developed curves in all the right places. He'd also admired her competitiveness with him—they sharpened each other as they tried to outdo one another.

That said, her total lack of interest in his charms had cooled that crush pretty quickly. He didn't need a prickly girlfriend he had to work to get. Not when the other girls were more than happy to be one of his many dates. He wasn't into relationships back then, just good times. Rawlston finished his coffee and sighed. But when he'd finally committed to a real relationship as an adult, it had ended in betrayal and divorce, ending the naval career he might have pursued and sending him back to ranching. Which wasn't a bad thing—a man could be alone out here day after day. He was okay with that.

His phone pinged with an incoming text, and he knew without a doubt it had to be Dahlia. She'd been blowing up his phone since they got back to Chatelaine, swearing him to secrecy repeatedly and updating him on her progress in divorcing him. He pulled out his phone and saw his guess was right.

Talked to an attorney yesterday afternoon, and he filled me in on what we need to do. Got time to meet today?

Sure. Why not? He'd planned on heading to the farm supply store anyway. He tapped his response.

Going to Longhorn Feed this morning. Coffee at the Daily Grind in two hours?

Her answer was immediate.

The sooner the better. See you there.

She was not only awake, but ready to roll this morning. Probably because she was so determined to end things with him.

The coffee shop was just across the two-lane highway from the feedstore. This was the "townie" side of Chatelaine—no mansions or resorts out here like there were in the ritzy Chatelaine Hills neighborhood on the other side of town. Just ranchers and the folks who worked at the mansions for the millionaires on the other end of Lake Chatelaine. This was blue-collar Chatelaine. *Dusty* blue collar. Rawlston slapped at his jeans to shake the dust off from loading bags of feed into the back of his dual-rear-wheel pickup truck.

This was his favorite side of town. He was successful enough that he could afford to hang out at the fancy LC Club on the water with all its tourists. But dressing up and listening to everyone brag about what they owned wasn't his idea of fun. He'd rather have coffee with the folks at the Daily Grind and talk ranching.

Once a modest home, the square, one-story building with a wide front porch had been converted to a restaurant back in the 1930s. The interior hadn't changed much since then, even as the place changed hands and formats a few times. Thirty years ago, it was reborn as a coffee shop that catered to ranchers, opening at six in the morning and closing in the early afternoon. Being right across the road from the feedstore made it the ideal spot for ranchers to stop by for a cup of strong coffee, something sweet and all of the best local gossip.

The shop was busy when he stepped inside, and he immediately spotted why. Beau Weatherly was at his corner table by the window, with a handful of people waiting for him. A small folding sign on the table read Free Life Advice. Rawlston checked his watch—the man's free advice time was running long today. He usually started at seven and answered people's questions until eight thirty or so. On the mornings when Beau was there, the Daily Grind would attract those who wanted advice and those who wanted to see who was asking for advice.

Beau was an interesting guy. The tall, gray-haired, stately gentleman was a salt-of-the-earth rancher with an unassuming demeanor who also happened to be a genius-level investor who'd made millions. His generosity had helped Chatelaine in many ways. He'd donated to numerous local charities, and had also quietly helped individual ranchers and local businesses when they needed it. That last part was just rumor, but Rawlston had heard it often enough to figure it was true. Not that Beau would ever admit it.

Beau's wife had died shortly after Rawlston arrived in Chatelaine, and Beau had been lost without her. He'd let his ranch slide, and word around town was that he'd stopped doing much with his investments. He just sat in his massive house and stared at the walls, ignoring friends as well as business.

After a year or so of sitting in limbo like that, he'd suddenly decided to give life advice to people for free at the coffee shop. He said that helping people was what his wife would have wanted him to do, so he answered people's questions on whatever topic they wanted to know about. Would it rain next week? Should they buy XYZ stock? Would they ever reconcile with their grown child? What should they cook for a family barbecue that weekend? Beau had earned a reputation for wisdom on all subjects.

Rawlston removed his hat and gave Beau a nod from the doorway. The whole thing was a little too woo-woo for him, but it didn't seem that Beau was hurting anyone, and if he made people feel better, what was the harm?

The coffee shop was small, with a few square tables and a counter along the back with wooden stools. There were more tables on the front porch. It was simple but cheery, with its whitewashed shiplap walls and red gingham curtains. They not only served the best coffee in the county, but also had a selection of bagels and pastries that went perfectly with that oversize mug of coffee. A glass case displayed desserts—it looked like today was cream pie day.

Dahlia was already here, at a table on the far side of the room with one of Daily Grind's giant red coffee mugs in front of her. Her long, blond hair was pulled into some sort of knot on the back of her neck. She was in a pair of stonewashed jeans and a flattering dark green top, with Western boots. She had her share of the Windham wealth, in addition to probably inheriting a good sum from her grandfather, Wendell Fortune.

Dahlia could not only afford the LC Club action, but she'd fit in there like a natural with her supermodel good looks and the aura of growing up rich wrapped around her. Her clothes said working rancher. But her ramrod straight posture, carefully manicured nails and that porcelain complexion screamed *I should be on a yacht somewhere*. She'd always been out of his league. And yet—he bit back a smile—she was his wife.

"I highly recommend the banana cream pie," he said as he slid into the chair across from her.

"For breakfast?" Dahlia made a face.

"Trust me." A wiry older woman hustled over to take his order. "Hey, Sylvie. I'll take a big coffee, black, and a slice of that banana cream pie with two forks."

"Sure thing, Rawlston honey. You sure you want to share?" Sylvie eyed Dahlia through narrowed eyes. Sylvie was a mother hen to regulars like him, and she'd probably never seen the Fortune heiress before. "You usually have no problem eating our pie all on your own."

Dahlia was staring daggers at him as Sylvie headed back to the counter.

"Why do I get the feeling she doesn't like me?"

He huffed out a laugh. "Sylvie? She just doesn't know you. And to be honest, you're not the first woman I've been here with. She has no problem expressing her distaste for most of them." Lifting a shoulder, he muttered, "Sylvie thinks I need to find a nice rancher woman for my bride."

Dahlia smiled. "Don't tell Sylvie, but…you kinda did."

"That's true. But you don't look like a rancher. You look like a movie star."

Her eyebrows arched high. "I'm in jeans and boots, and I started the day in my brother's horse barn, checking on his favorite mare. I also have thirty sheep arriving later today, with more on the way. That's not exactly an A-lister lifestyle."

"I'm not saying you're not the real deal. I'm just saying you don't *look* like the real deal. You look like…" *A vision.* He blinked. High school had been a long time ago, but she still didn't want him. Time to focus. Sylvie saved the day by bringing a towering slice of banana cream pie to the table, along with his coffee.

"Extra strong, just the way you like it." That meant she'd added a shot of espresso.

"Thanks, Sylvie. Oh, we need another fork." She'd only brought one. She grumbled something and pulled the other out of her apron pocket and put it in front of Dahlia. Sylvie had seen him here with other women, but she'd never once seen him share his pie. "Sylvie, this is Dahlia Fortune. She's part of the Fortune Family Ranch, and she's starting a sheepherding operation there. She's great with horses, too. Won the junior state barrel racing championship back in high school."

Sylvie put her hand on her hip and reassessed Dahlia. For some reason Rawlston needed the waitress to know the woman sitting across from him wasn't a one-night stand of his. She was a rancher. And, secret or not, she was his *wife*. He wouldn't have her dismissed. Dahlia stared right back at the older woman, not defiant but not intimidated, either. Finally, Sylvie smiled, looking between the two of them at the table.

"Okay, then. Welcome to Chatelaine, Miss Fortune. Your momma has been in here a couple of times. She seems like good people."

"She's the best." As soon as Sylvie moved on to a different table, Dahlia slid a large manila envelope across the table toward him. "Annulment papers. Sign them."

Chapter Four

"Way to change the subject, Dolly." Rawlston's voice was light, but there was tension around his eyes. He couldn't possibly be surprised, Dahlia thought. They both wanted this, and it was the reason they were sitting in this coffee shop so early in the morning.

"Stop calling me that. Someone's going to hear you and then it will stick and I am *not* anyone's Dolly." Her fingers were still resting on the envelope for some reason, and she slid them off. "The annulment or divorce or whatever will take a month or so to finalize, but if we start the process now, no one needs to know. It'll just... go away."

He was still staring at the envelope, as if it held something terrible.

"Rawlston?" She leaned forward, lowering her voice even further. "We can't dillydally here. That whole night was one big, drunken, foolish mistake, and we have to fix it. I have a *boyfriend*. This could ruin everything that Carter and I have together."

It wasn't until she said Carter's name out loud that Rawlston looked up. He took another bite of the pie, then gestured for her to do the same. She rolled her eyes and did it, just to humor him.

Holy banana tree. This was the best pie of *any* kind that Dahlia could remember eating. Rich but not too rich, sweet but not sickeningly so, creamy without being heavy, with just the right amount of banana flavor. She blinked, then noticed Rawlston's quick, slanted grin as he watched her. Was he trying to sidetrack her from the annulment papers with *pie*?

"Yes, fine, it's very good pie. Are you happy? Now please look at the paperwork. The firm I hired sent a list of all the reasons people can legally choose to annul a Vegas wedding, and broke down the whole process. The only thing we're signing today is the agreement to retain their services for the annulment, and—"

"What *do* you and Carter have?"

"What?" The question came from left field.

"You said this could ruin everything you and Carter have together. Are you two that serious?"

"I…" She realized her mouth was hanging open and snapped it shut. "I don't see where that's any of your business."

"Well, you *are* my wife, so—"

"Shh! I swear you're trying to let every gossip in here know what we did!" She was hissing the words at him. "Carter and I have been dating for six months."

Rawlston sat back in his seat. "Congratulations. But I asked what you *have*. Are you in business together?" He frowned. "You haven't invested any money with him, have you?"

"I don't know why you care, but no. I haven't invested with Carter."

It wasn't for the lack of opportunity. Carter had asked her for money more than once, either as a straightforward investment in his company or to help fund his political action committee for the campaign that hadn't been announced yet. But Dahlia had always declined. Money complicated things, and she didn't want things to become muddled between her and Carter. It was one of the few relationships in her life that was *un*complicated. Two grown-ups who were compatible. No drama. No fuss.

Rawlston nodded thoughtfully. "So you two *are* serious?"

"We're getting there, yes." Carter had hinted pretty heavily that he was going diamond shopping. Which meant there'd be a wedding proposal shortly after he got home. The idea didn't make her heart go pitter-patter or anything, but Carter was a good guy. He'd had a hard time adjusting to her move from Cactus Grove to Chatelaine, but he would come to see that it made her happy. That said, it *had* rubbed her the wrong way when he'd laughed at her announcement that she was going to raise sheep here. He'd called her Bo Peep. She knew he would come around on that, too, in due time. She'd jokingly told him it would be good for his campaign if he had a rancher girlfriend, and he'd responded by saying he'd have the campaign run a focus group on it. Romantic? No. But he was just trying to be practical. She understood that.

"So you're going to tell him about us, then?" Rawlston took another bite of pie, chewing it while waiting for her response.

"There is no *us*," she snapped.

"The marriage certificate on my desk at home says otherwise."

Her teeth clenched. "What I tell him or not is none of your business. God, Rawlston, you and I haven't spoken in years and now you think you can tell me what to do just because…" She looked around the quiet coffee shop and lowered her voice. "Because we got drunk in Vegas and made a mistake. Mistakes can be erased, and that's exactly what will happen once you sign the paperwork and we get the annulment."

She tapped her fingers on the manila envelope, but his gaze remained on her face, his expression impossible to read. Finally he shook his head and picked up the envelope.

"You're right—it was a pretty big mistake. But if you're in that serious of a relationship, it seems like you'd want to tell him. I thought good relationships were based on honesty. But hey, maybe I'm wrong."

Her conscience twitched just a little. She had to tread carefully with Carter. She needed to pick the right time, and frame it in a way that wouldn't upset him. Did that bode well for a long-term relationship? Maybe not, but then again, being thoughtful about if and when to share information made sense. And, in truth, she had no idea how she was going to explain her Vegas wedding in a way that would make it seem like good news for either one of them.

"I'm not saying I won't ever tell him. It's probably something we'll laugh about years from now. I'm just saying I'm not going to spring it on him as soon as he gets off the plane in a few weeks—*Guess what, honey? I accidentally got married while you were gone!*"

A slow grin curved one corner of Rawlston's mouth, and his gray-blue eyes darkened. "Don't forget the ac-cidentally-slept-with-the-guy part."

An odd tingle danced across her skin. She only remembered snippets of that night, but the snippets were hot. Wild. Funny. Tender. The sex couldn't possibly have been that good. It must have been her imagination filling in memory gaps. But there was something about his heated gaze right now that felt very familiar. She needed to deflect this conversation.

"No good can possibly come from talking about that night. With Carter *or* with you. Let's just…forget it."

"Forget it?" His voice was level, but she heard a mix of humor and disbelief behind it.

"Look, it happened. We can't deny it. Thank God we were aware enough to use protection." She swallowed hard. "We have to deal with the marriage part, but we do not need to relive the rest of that night. It's…it's humiliating for me."

The heat and humor vanished from his eyes in an instant. He sat forward and put his hand over hers, then glanced around and slid his fingers back so that just their fingertips were touching.

"We had no idea we were getting blackout drunk from that damn fruit punch, so our judgment was obviously impaired. But *what* we did…at least what I remember…" he almost smiled but seemed to catch himself "…we were two adults having safe and rather spectacular sex."

Dahlia's face heated. In fact, her whole body did—a flush that rose from her belly to her cheeks. He thought she was spectacular? She gave herself a mental shake. It didn't matter what Rawlston thought. That night was *never* going to happen again.

"Hey…" His gruff voice made her meet his gaze. "I was out of line, telling you how to handle things with Carter. I'll support whatever you want to do, including never telling a soul for the rest of our lives. But just so you know… I'll *never* forget it."

If she thought she was warm before, her skin was on fire now. From his words. His steady gaze. The touch of his fingers against hers. Which was ridiculous. She snatched her hand away, then picked up her fork and stabbed the pie slice so hard that some of the whipped cream topping sprayed on the table. She took the bite in her mouth and sat back, trying to regain a semblance of balance.

"I can't help what goes on inside your brain, Rawlston, but no one can know about this. Just…sign those papers and get them back to me so we can get the annulment started, okay?" She glanced at her watch and pushed away from the table. "I've got to get back to the ranch. My sheep arrive in a few hours."

"How'd the family take that news?" he asked.

"Some didn't care. Some did. But I didn't get any pushback."

As long as she didn't count her brother Nash's loud insistence that sheep were not moneymakers and that she'd made an "impulsive" decision. She'd dealt with her father's skepticism about her dreams her entire life, so she hadn't let Nash's opinion bother her. If anything, it was extra motivation to bring her plan to fruition. She'd learned to use men's opinions of her as fuel. Dad didn't think she should barrel race? She became state champion barrel racer. Dad and her brothers called her "contrary," but she didn't see it that way. She simply didn't like anyone telling her what to do.

She turned to leave, but Rawlston stopped her. "My

father's having a big cookout this weekend. You should come."

"As what, your *wife*?" She shook her head, but he answered before she could continue.

"As my *neighbor*. You could meet some of the locals. If you really want to get this wool business going, you'll need to have customers." He tapped the envelope. "Maybe I'll have this signed by then."

She wasn't sure what to think about the invite, but she knew what she thought about that paperwork. "You could sign that right now. It's just to get things rolling."

"My daddy taught me not to sign anything I haven't read carefully. Dad's barbecue is at three o'clock on Sunday. I'm sure he'd like to see you there."

"I'll think about it." She left Rawlston to finish the pie and drove back to the Fortune Family Ranch.

Home, even if it didn't feel that way yet.

Dahlia sat back in the brightly patterned chaise lounge with a heavy sigh.

Her twin, Sabrina, started to laugh. "Life as a rancher getting to you already?"

They were sitting on Dahlia's spacious back deck, overlooking a long, narrow lap pool and beyond that, Lake Chatelaine. A timber-framed roof extended out from the log house to shield most of the deck from the sun, and a large fan hung down from the peak to keep the hot air moving. With the temperature over a hundred degrees for the third day in a row, the fan wasn't helping much. She took a sip of her sangria, looking over the rim at Sabrina.

They weren't identical twins, but their looks were very

similar. Both were tall, slim, blond and blue-eyed. They had what their father had once described as "Betty Boop" faces—heart-shaped with large eyes and pouty lips. He'd assured them from childhood that the world would fall at their feet at just one look from them, as if their appearance was their best feature. Casper envisioned them successfully married—as in married to a rich man—not as successful individuals with plans of their own.

Sabrina was more of a numbers girl. She'd been an accountant at a children's charity in Dallas, and was now managing the finances for the Fortune Family Ranch. Dahlia, on the other hand, understood numbers just fine, but didn't want to spend her life looking at them.

"What?" Sabrina asked. "Why are you staring at me?"

Dahlia set her glass down on the teak side table. "I don't know. I guess I'm wondering how we got here, living in neighboring log houses on a lake and running a ranch."

Sabrina nodded. "It's been a wild year, hasn't it?" She paused. "Any regrets yet?"

Other than marrying Rawlston Ames?

"Uh…no." She shifted in her seat, adjusting her sunglasses. "I still stumble over my new last name since we changed them. But the houses on the ranch are very nice, and I'm beginning to be able to find my way around the ranch and around town. The sheep are settling in their pastures. And most importantly, Mom seems *really* happy here in Chatelaine."

"I am glad for Mom, but you know how I felt about the name thing. Nothing against the other Fortunes, but a name change was a big deal for me." Sabrina had always been closer to their father than Dahlia had. "But I have to agree that these houses are pretty sweet."

When Wendy Fortune bought the ranch for her children, there were already six luxurious log homes along the lakeshore, in addition to the large main house where she lived. These weren't cabins—they were basically waterfront mansions with log exteriors. Most had a contemporary feel, with cathedral ceilings, open floor plans and walls of windows facing the lake. Like Dahlia's, the others had big, multilevel decks in back, with pools and/or docks on the water so they could have boats if they wanted.

"This house is a major upgrade from my old condo in Cactus Springs, but let's face it—Chatelaine is not Dallas by a long shot. It's growing on me, though." Even though she'd moved here with five siblings, Dahlia felt the place offered new opportunities for her individually. People didn't know her here, so she wasn't saddled with their expectations.

Back in Cactus Grove, everyone had assumed she'd want to do something with horses—raise them, train them, race them. No one took the time to learn that she loved creating things with wool, or that she'd started dreaming of raising her own sheep.

But here, no one blinked an eye at the news. She was a Fortune, but there were Fortunes everywhere in Texas. It honestly didn't carry the pressure of being Casper Windham's daughter in Cactus Grove, where he'd been more infamous than adored.

Dahlia sat up. "Want me to heat some carnitas? I picked them up from that little Mexican place on the far side of town, along with some chicken taquitos."

Sabrina nodded then followed her into the kitchen, with its hickory cupboards and swirling brown quartz countertops. The four-bedroom house was a little masculine for Dahlia's taste. There was a lot of brown, but she hoped to change that when she had a chance to do some redecorating. Which wouldn't be anytime soon, since she had another truckload of sheep arriving the following week. Her dream was becoming a reality, and so was the workload. She warmed the food and set out a basket of chips with salsa and guacamole.

They ate inside to enjoy the air-conditioning, talking about the sheep and their latest wool projects. Sabrina loved to knit and crochet, and she often tackled some of the toughest patterns. Dahlia's preferred woolcraft was needle felting, where she basically painted scenes with wool across a wool background or on an embroidery hoop. Her rebellious streak carried over to her art, so working with patterns left her feeling constrained. With needle felting, she created her own vision and could alter it as needed.

"So how soon until I can get my wool directly from you?" Sabrina asked, pouring more sangria into their glasses from the pitcher on the counter. Dahlia couldn't help thinking of the night she and Rawlston kept refilling their glasses with spiked punch, and how it ended with them married. And in bed. She straightened abruptly.

"What?" She tried to remember what her twin had asked. "Oh, I might do some shearing this fall, but most of it will be done next spring. Bender gave me contact information for some good shearers up near Waco, and they have me on their spring schedule."

Bender—his real name was Bobby—Grant was one

of the ranch hands for the main barns. He worked the cattle now, but also had a lot of experience as a younger man raising and caring for sheep. Her brother, Nash, acting as foreman of the ranch, was in charge of the workers, and he'd agreed Bender could work for Dahlia on a part-time basis to help with her sheep. Bender had been on the Fortune ranch property far longer than any of the Fortunes had, and longer than the previous owners, too. He'd spent most of his life here, living alone in one of the trailers clustered together near the main barns and office. He was a quiet guy, but he seemed genuinely happy to be in charge of the sheep herd.

"Don't worry about wool, though," Dahlia continued. "I'm buying it in bulk from Sally Mathison, the woman I bought some of the herd from, so I'll have wool for you. But it will be raw, not spun yet. And not dyed, although I may start playing with dyeing over the winter." Her dream was to sell not only her art and Sabrina's clothing items, but also to sell spun wool to other crafters.

Dahlia was clearing the dishes when Sabrina took her by the wrist. "Okay, sis. What's going on?"

"W-what do you mean?"

"My twin-sense is going off like crazy. Something is different with you, and it's not just the changes we've all been through lately." Sabrina pursed her lips. "You're acting funny, like you're not telling me something. What gives?"

Dahlia pulled away. "I don't know what you're talking about. Everything's fine. *I'm* fine." She glanced at her bare left hand, where a wedding band had been not that long ago.

"Does it have anything to do with Rawlston Ames?"

"I…no… I…*what*?" The mention of his name short-circuited her brain.

Sabrina stared hard for a moment, her eyes narrowed. "So it *is* him. Someone said they saw you two at the Daily Grind the other morning, and that you left in a hurry. The last I knew, you two were arch rivals, but high school was a long time ago. So I'll ask again. What's going on?"

Dahlia was still frozen. Her mind was spinning, but it wasn't conjuring any words to say. Just images of Raw-lston—striding across the exhibition hall in his Stetson, laughing with her at the secluded booth near the punch bowl, swooping in for a kiss in the hot pink chapel, slowly sliding her top from her shoulders in his suite—

"Holy… Are you *blushing*?" Sabrina stood and came around the kitchen island. "I didn't even know you two were in contact with each other. What did he do? What did *you* do?"

"Nothing!" she insisted, trying to turn away, but Sabrina stopped her. Dahlia couldn't look her twin in the eye and lie. So she tried to tell some *little* truths in order to avoid the big truth. "We bumped into each other in Las Vegas, and spent a little time catching up, that's all. Did you know he owns the neighboring ranch to ours? Anyway, we talked about my plans for the sheep, and he…" She was losing track of her own story. "And he… wanted information. When we saw each other at the Daily Grind, I gave him that…information. And then I left, because that was the day the first load of sheep arrived, remember?" She chewed her lip, knowing she hadn't sounded very convincing.

"So you spent time catching up. In Vegas." Sabrina

paused, then brightened. "Oh my God, did you and Carter break up? Do you *like* Rawlston now?"

"No, and definitely no. Carter and I are still together." Even if she was technically married to someone else. Minor detail. Totally fixable. "And I do *not* like Rawlston. I mean, I don't hate him, but he's....inconsequential."

Her twin smiled smugly. "You only use big, fancy words like *inconsequential* when you're nervous. What really happened when you guys met up in Vegas?"

Dahlia stared straight up at the ceiling, trying and failing to find a way out of this. But she couldn't hide the truth from Sabrina.

"We accidentally got married."

Sabrina's mouth fell open. "I'm sorry, did you just say you *married* Rawlston Ames in Las Vegas?"

"What in the hell did I just miss?"

Sabrina and Dahlia turned to see their younger sister, Jade, standing near the front door. Her eyes were round with shock. *Perfect.* Dahlia muttered a curse. Why hadn't she at least *tried* to lie? Jade rushed to join them in the kitchen.

"Tell me everything! Right now. Does this mean Carter's out of the picture?"

Her sisters had never hidden their disdain for Carter. Jade once said he was a miniature version of their father, and that Dahlia had some sort of reverse Oedipus complex that drew her to him. Total nonsense, of course.

"Carter is *not* out of the picture. In fact, I'm pretty sure he's going to propose when he gets back from Europe."

Sabrina snorted. "Won't that be a little crowded if you're already married to Rawlston? And what do you mean, you *accidentally* married him?"

After a heavy sigh, she gestured toward the island. Her sisters sat in rapt attention as she gave them the highlights of her so-called wedding night. The spiked punch, the hours of conversation, the barely remembered trip to the chapel, waking up in his bed—

"Wait," Jade interrupted. "Are you saying you two actually consummated this accidental wedding? Like you just took a wrong turn into the chapel and then *oops*, your clothes fell off?"

"How was it?" Sabrina took Dahlia's hands in hers. "He's matured into one hot man. Was the sex good?"

"I don't know! We were basically blackout drunk by then." The truth was, she was remembering more and more pieces of that night and they were all very, very good. But there were some things even her twin didn't need to know.

"So *now* what?" Jade asked.

"Now we get an annulment, just as quickly as possible." Hopefully Rawlston had signed the attorney paperwork so they could get started. Tomorrow was that cookout he'd mentioned was happening at his father's place. Maybe she should go after all, just to get the promised signatures from him. She straightened, giving her sisters her most threatening look. "No one else can know about this. I'm serious. Do not tell a soul. Got it?"

"So…" Sabrina started "…you're just going to quietly end the marriage and not tell anyone? Not even Carter?"

"That's the plan. There's apparently a whole branch of Nevada law built around ending Vegas weddings, and the process is pretty straightforward. That's why we met at the Daily Grind—so I could give him some preliminary documents to sign."

Jade squinted, looking thoughtful. "You sure you want to do that? Rawlston's a catch. He's a huge improvement on *Carter.*" Her mouth twisted when she said Carter's name, making her feelings very clear.

"Yes, I'm sure." Dahlia rolled her eyes. "I barely *know* Rawlston, other than how annoying he was in high school. Carter and I have been dating for six months now, and we're really good together, so give it a rest, Jade."

"*Really good together?* What does that even mean?" Jade waved her hand in dismissal. "It's hardly a declaration of undying love."

Dahlia frowned into her glass. Jade had a point. It didn't sound quite right, considering she was hoping to marry Carter.

But…if she truly *loved* Carter, she had a feeling all the alcohol in the world wouldn't have been enough to get her to marry another man in Las Vegas. And that man, Rawlston Ames, wouldn't be haunting her dreams the way he had been all week.

Chapter Five

"**D**ad, I'm not trying to tell you how to grill, but—"

Rawlston's father shook a pair of metal tongs in his direction. "Don't ever approach another man's grill with unsolicited advice, son. I taught you better than that."

Keith Ames was a big man, and people tended to listen to him. But Rawlston wasn't "people" and he nudged his father to the side. "I know a thing or two about steak, and I'm telling you the flame's too high. You're going to end up serving shoe leather."

His dad nudged him right back, rocking him back on his heels. "Boy, I was grillin' steak before you were a glimmer in my eye. I'm putting a sear on, then I'll lower the heat and close the lid. It'll be fine. Go bother someone else."

Rawlston shook his head with a low chuckle. He hadn't seen his dad this animated in a while. They were just playing with each other, of course. They'd been razzing each other about grilling for years. But since Rawlston's mother died five years ago, Dad hadn't been as jovial as he seemed to be today. There was a brightness to his smile and a twinkle in his eyes that hadn't been there in a long time.

The veranda surrounding the pool behind Dad's home

was filling with people. This cookout was looking like an event, and Rawlston wondered what the occasion was. Dad had been very mysterious about the whole thing, just saying he had something to announce to his friends and family. Rawlston figured his father was going to take a trip somewhere and just wanted to let people know. He'd been talking about a fishing trip to Alaska. But this was a bigger and more well-heeled crowd than Dad usually hosted.

"What is this big announcement about, again?" he asked. Dad just laughed, never looking up from the thick slabs of steak on the grill.

"Nice try, kid. I told you—it's a surprise. I don't want to tell the story over and over, so everyone who might care was invited. And even a few I didn't invite." He gave Rawlston a sideways glance. "That pretty Fortune lady said *you* invited her."

Dahlia? His eyes immediately scanned the people milling around with cocktails and hors d'oeuvres, provided by servers. Other than his precious steaks, Dad had left the rest of it to the caterers.

Dad snorted. "So it's true. I remember her from when you were in high school. Are you and her an item now?"

Well, they would be if anyone found out about their marriage. "No, Dad. She has the ranch next to mine and I told her this would be a good place to meet more Chatelaine residents." He gave his father a pointed look. "And that's all there is."

"You're slipping, son. She's a looker, and I heard she's smart as a whip, too. The two of you would be—"

"Don't even think about playing matchmaker, old man. Dahlia and I are friends." And barely that.

"That's too bad. It's about time you found a good woman and settled down."

His jaw went tight. "I tried that, remember?"

Dad basted the steaks with melted butter and herbs. Aromatic smoke rose up from the grill. "I said find a *good* woman. They're out there, you know. Everyone has a someone, even if they haven't met them yet."

"What is it with you and all the touchy-feely talk lately?" His father had started acting differently in the past month or so—smiling, whistling, and waxing poetic about life and romance.

"Maybe I'm gettin' wiser in my old age, son. Maybe I have a newfound appreciation for the mysteries of life and the rhythms of love." Dad was waving the basting brush in the air. "And maybe you could learn a thing or two from listening to my *touchy-feely* talk. Oh, there she is."

Rawlston followed Dad's gaze to the veranda above them and saw Dahlia staring back. She wore a gauzy skirt and top in shades of beige and soft blue. Her hair was long and straight, looking almost white in the Texas sun. She gave a quick wave with her fingers. He excused himself from his father, ignoring Dad's smug laughter. No matter what his old man might think, there were no cupid's arrows between Dahlia and him. But he had to admit there *was* a pull there, drawing him to her.

"Rawlston." Her voice was low and thick.

"Dahlia." He couldn't help smiling at her. "I'm glad you could make it."

She glanced around. "You and your dad are the only people I know here."

"Your brother Ridge is supposed to stop by, and Arlo might, too. I saw them the other day and invited them."

She arched a brow. "You seem very invested in helping us Fortunes get to meet people in Chatelaine."

"Well, you're all trying to get settled, and they *are* my brothers-in-law now." He couldn't resist teasing her.

Her eyes narrowed dangerously. "Stop it!" she hissed. "We are *not* family. In fact, the only reason I came today was to pick up the attorney papers I gave you. You've signed them, right?"

He hadn't, actually. He'd read them, then slid them right back into the envelope. As she'd assured him the other day, the papers weren't a big deal. It was just an agreement to be clients of the law firm for the purpose of annulling their marriage. Signing them would allow the attorneys to start the legal process. But still…he hadn't signed.

"They're out in my truck," he finally said, not exactly answering her question.

"Good. The sooner we get things moving, the better. Carter's back from Europe in a few weeks, and I want this as close to finished as possible." She looked around the spacious yard and pool area. "Your father's place is nice."

He followed her gaze. "Dad and Mom planned to move to Chatelaine Hills together. This little hobby ranch was supposed to be their retirement home. Then she got sick and they stayed near Dallas for her treatments. She designed this place, but never had the chance to enjoy it. Dad moved here shortly after we lost her, and I followed a year later." After his divorce. His voice dropped. "Mom would have loved seeing all these people here."

"I was really sorry to hear about her passing. She was always so sweet."

"She was, thanks." He met her gaze. "I remember seeing you at the memorial. Thanks for that, too."

He'd been wrapped up taking care of his father and handling his own grief back then. He didn't remember if he spoke to Dahlia at all after the service.

"Your dad looks like he's doing well."

He glanced down to where Dad was grilling what looked like the last batch of Angus steaks. Leave it to him to make it clear he preferred his own Black Angus beef over Rawlston's Brahman cattle. But his father *did* look good. He had a beer in his hand, and he was laughing at something Beau Weatherly was saying. He and Beau had both lost their wives, and the experience had created a bond between the men that had deepened into friendship.

At that moment, Rufus Wilkins walked up to Rawlston and Dahlia. The older man owned a ranch a little farther out from Chatelaine, where he raised some of the best quarter horses in Texas, which was saying something. Rawlston started to introduce him to Dahlia, but of course, they already knew each other. She'd worked for Rufus as a groom and trainer on the racetrack, and the mare she'd won so many barrel racing awards with had come from his ranch. As the two began talking horses, Rawlston excused himself and went to catch up with another rancher. He mingled and socialized through dinner, and so did Dahlia.

She was never completely out of his line of sight as she made the rounds, introducing herself and chatting with her new neighbors. She didn't need his help with networking—she was a natural. Dahlia put her hand on some woman's shoulder and laughed, her hair tossed back and her eyes bright with humor. He caught her eye and, instead of the coolness she generally aimed his way, her gaze was warm and relaxed. Moments later, she made her way through the crowd toward him.

Everyone was nibbling on desserts now, and cocktails had been replaced with coffee and brandy. His father was up on the edge of the veranda, and he clinked his spoon against his glass for attention. Rawlston had almost forgotten there was an announcement coming. He gave a quick nod to Dahlia as his father began to speak to the hushed group.

"Ladies and gentlemen, thank you for coming to my little picnic today."

Someone shouted out from near the pool. "Picnic? More like a feast!"

Keith Ames grinned and held his glass up in a mock toast. "I'm glad you enjoyed it, Tommy. I'll confess I threw this party for purely selfish reasons. I have news to share, and I only want to share it once."

Rawlston frowned. That made it sound like bad news. Was his father ill? A ripple of unease went through the partiers, as if some of them felt the same way.

"No, no," Dad said, "it's nothing like that. This is good news, but it's also news that's going to get tongues wagging, so I want to get ahead of the grapevine and give you the facts straight up." He paused, a smile slowly spreading on his face. "I've met someone."

This time, the ripple going through the audience was one of excitement. But Rawlston went very still. He'd had no idea Dad had started dating. In all honesty, he didn't *hate* the idea. He didn't want his father to be alone the rest of his life. But if he was making an announcement this grand…

"And I'm getting married." There was a collective gasp. Dad's smile deepened. "And no, none of you have met her. Because *I* haven't met her yet…at least not face-to-face."

"He's kidding, right?" Dahlia asked softly. "Is this his way of saying he's going to start dating or that he *has* been dating?"

"I haven't a freakin' clue," Rawlston growled. He was on edge, but also concerned. Dad's health might be okay, but was his mind starting to go? He and Dahlia weren't the only ones asking questions, and his father raised a hand to silence everyone.

"Here's the deal. I stumbled across a dating app that's just for farmers and ranchers. I wasn't looking to date as much as just…find someone to talk to. The evenings get long and quiet around here, and I missed discussing the news of the day, or the workings of the ranch, with a woman. Ever since Kathy died, I've been mighty lonely." He looked at Rawlston. "My son and my friends have done their best, but they can't be here all the time, and I don't want them to be. They have their own lives."

Dad cleared his throat with a cough. "Anyway, I had correspondence with a few different women, and it was nice, but it wasn't until I met JoAnn that everything just shifted for me. She and I have been texting and talking for five months now, and she has made my life so much brighter and lighter. JoAnn's a widow from Vermont. She and her late husband had a dairy farm for forty years, so she knows all about livestock and the farming life."

He paused, then rushed ahead again. "I proposed and she said yes. She's moving to Chatelaine next week, and I expect every single person here to welcome her with open arms." He stared right at Rawlston on that final sentence and remained fixed on him. "JoAnn and I hope to be married by the end of August. She's kind and funny and adventurous, and... I like her very much. I want her in my life, which means she'll be in your lives, too."

"Oh, wow," Dahlia breathed. She rested her hand on his arm. "Did you know anything about—"

"Not even a hint." Rawlston had very rarely in his life ever been angry with his father, but right now all he could see was red. Why hadn't Dad said anything? What if this lady was a con artist? What if she was just after Dad's money? How *dare* he just move some random stranger into what was supposed to have been Rawlston's *mother's* home.

"Rawlston..." There was warning in Dahlia's voice now, as if she felt his rising rage. "Look at him. Your dad seems happy. Don't spoil his moment by—"

He pulled away, looking at her in shock. "You, of all people, shouldn't be talking about stopping someone from rushing into a disastrous wedding." She glanced around to see if anyone heard him, her face paling. He dropped his voice, but it was still vibrating with anger. "This sham of a marriage isn't going to happen. If it *does*, I'll end it just as fast as you're ending ours."

Rawlston stormed away, doing his best to keep his expression neutral as everyone began applauding his father's ridiculous news. He drew Dad away from the crowd of well-wishers as quickly and quietly as possible, finally wrangling him into the study and closing the door with more force than he'd intended.

"Easy, son."

Rawlston stood for a moment, head down, hand on the doorknob, trying to compose himself. When he thought he was ready, he slowly turned to face his father.

"Are you okay, Dad? Do you need to talk to your doctor? Have some blood work done? Maybe get some pills for depression or an altered mental state? Because there's clearly something wrong if you think you're marrying some random woman you've never even met face-to-face."

Dad smiled. "I had a full physical last month, and the doctor said I'm in prime condition for my age. There's nothing wrong with my brain, either, but thanks for your concern." His expression sobered. "And JoAnn isn't just 'some woman.' She and I have been corresponding for months. We've been video-chatting before bed almost every night for weeks. We know things about each other that no one else in our lives knows. Including you." His father leaned back against his oak desk. "I know every book and movie she loves. She knows I'm obsessed with all those *Law and Order* shows, and she's wild about *Yellowstone*. I had to make it very clear to her that I am not Kevin Costner."

Dad winked, but Rawlston didn't return the smile. "She writes poetry and she likes to grow flowers. And she loves history. She wants to take me to *Greece*, of all places, just so she can visit some old temples or something. Son, she's made my life... Well, she's made it a life worth living again. I actually look *forward* to getting up every morning now, and I haven't felt that way since we lost your mother."

"And what *about* my mother?" Rawlston demanded, his voice rising. "What about your wife?"

"Watch your tone, son." Dad's eyes went flint hard. "Your mother isn't here anymore. I mean, she'll *always* be here—I loved her more than the air I breathed. But I can't be alone anymore, Rawlston. I can't do it. I'm asking you to understand that."

"And you couldn't tell me this was all happening?"

"I *could* have, but I chose not to. Look at how you're reacting right now. I didn't want your disapproval coloring how I saw JoAnn. I wanted it to just be me and her for as long as possible, without the outside world pushing us one direction or another."

Rawlston paced the room, rubbing the back of his neck in agitation. "Okay, fine. You want companionship. That's fair. First, there are plenty of women in Chatelaine—hell, in all of *Texas*—that would be willing to be your companion. Be on your arm at parties. Go to dinner with you. You didn't need to reach all the way to New England for that. Secondly, it's okay to like a woman. It's okay to like *this* woman. That doesn't mean you have to rush into *marriage*. Why can't you just take things slow?"

Keith Ames nodded, then straightened, making sure he was looking Rawlston right in the eye. "Man to man? I'm not getting any younger, son. And I miss having a woman in my life…for more than just friendship."

"I get it." Rawlston held up his hand. "But why do you need to *marry* her? Marriage is painful and complicated to get out of. Trust me, I know." He was referring to Dahlia, but Dad thought he meant Lana.

"I know your one experience with marriage wasn't great," Dad started. "But I believe in marriage. You think I'm dishonoring your mother by marrying JoAnn, but I'm actually honoring the things Kathy and I valued in life—fidelity, commitment, partnership."

"You can have those things without getting *married*. Bring this woman to Texas…call her your girlfriend if you want. Have a good time. And when it's over, send her back to Vermont with only what she came here with, and not a penny more."

"Worried about your inheritance, Rawlston?" There was a warning edge to his tone.

"Dad, I don't need your inheritance. But *you* do. And for all you know, this stranger is thinking a lonely old man is an easy mark."

He knew the words were a mistake the minute they crossed his lips. His father was only sixty-five, and he'd earned an MBA from the University of Texas, as well as a degree in finance. He'd never been a stupid man, but he *was* a proud one. "Dad, I didn't mean—"

"Oh, yes, you did. Don't BS me now that you've spoken the words out loud. Own them." Keith Ames didn't often intimidate his son, but right now he was so angry and tense that it took all Rawlston had in him not to step back. His father poked him hard in the chest. "You think I'm some doddering old fool who's been hoodwinked by a dame. Nice to know my own son thinks so little of me."

"Dad—"

"Be quiet. Just—" he sighed heavily, then patted his hand on the spot he'd just poked "—be quiet. I know you're trying to look out for me, son." His voice softened. "And I blindsided you with this, mainly because

I was afraid of having this exact conversation. But that time gave me a chance to be sure without any pressure. I'm *sure*, Rawlston. JoAnn is a good woman, and I want her to be my wife. Not my gal pal. Not my partner in the sheets. My *wife*."

Rawlston blinked and glanced away, taking a step back. While he couldn't wrap his head around his father's decision, he couldn't fight him anymore, either. He started muttering to himself, eyes tightly closed as he tried to come to terms with it all. "It's been quite a month, with the two of us getting married and probably the two of us racing toward divorce, too." Divorce. Annulment. What was the difference?

"What did you say?"

Uh-oh. Had he just said that out loud? He cleared his throat loudly. "What? Nothing. I just hope your marriage lasts longer than…" He coughed. "Than the summer."

His father's eyes narrowed on Rawlston. "You said the 'two of *us* getting married.' What the heck did you mean by that?"

There was a long beat of silence in the room, although the party seemed to be going strong outside. Music was playing and there was a steady hum of laughter and conversation. He did his best to look his dad in the eye and act as if nothing was awkward at all. He failed.

"Remember when I was in Las Vegas a week ago?"

"Yeah." Realization began to dawn on Dad's face. "Aw, hell. You didn't marry some showgirl or something, did you?"

"Worse. I married Dahlia Fortune."

It was hard to track all the emotions that crossed his father's face. Shock. Disbelief. Concern. And then…

absolute, unadulterated delight. Dad let out a laugh that morphed into a whoop of celebration as he clapped his hands together and started laughing for real.

"Son, I swear to God if you're pulling my leg, I'll take you out behind the barn like I did when you were ten. But if you're *not*, then *praise Jesus*, because that's the best news I've heard since JoAnn accepted my proposal!"

Rawlston gestured for Dad to be quiet. "Keep it down! No one knows, and no one *can* know. It was a mistake, and we're fixing it."

"Why? Dahlia's a great gal."

"Dahlia's dating Carter Powers, and she intends to *keep* dating him." Maybe even marry the jerk.

His father's face fell. "Really? Well, that's disappointing. She's clearly never done business with the guy."

Keith Ames had been pulled into one of Carter's so-called investments, which had basically been a well-disguised Ponzi scheme. By the time his father realized it was all smoke and mirrors, he'd lost over two hundred thousand dollars. It would have been a lot more, but Dad had pulled his money out when he saw the red flags. Carter had mocked him for not having *the guts to invest with the big dogs*.

His father sat on the corner of his desk again while Rawlston filled him in on the Las Vegas story—the spiked punch, the wedding veil that lit up, the bright pink chapel and the legally binding marriage certificate sitting on his dresser when they woke up the next morning.

Dad thought for a moment, then his smile returned. "She can't get serious with Carter as long as she's married to you, right?" The same thought had crossed Rawlston's mind. "So why not *stay* married a while longer?

You'd be doing her a favor in the long run, and hell, you might just find the two of you are a good match. Who knows, you might fall in love and stay married for *real*." He gave an exaggerated shrug. "After all, love and matrimony are in the air for the Ames men this month."

Rawlston felt his anger flaring again. He was mad at himself for even being tempted to consider the crazy idea. He was mad at his father for marrying a total stranger. He was mad at a world that seemed determined to convince him there was anything *good* about marriage. Because there *wasn't*. He'd given up his navy career for Lana and she'd left him anyway. And even if he *did* believe in marriage at all—which he did not—he was currently married to someone who didn't even want him. He'd already had *one* marriage like that. He'd be damned if he'd consider a *second*. He turned his back on his father and jerked open the door.

"Rawl—"

He slammed the door shut behind him, refusing to listen to any more of his father's nonsense. Marriage was for suckers. It was a long con that ended in broken dreams.

Chapter Six

Dahlia had been hanging around the living room, worried about Rawlston's confrontation with his father. He'd obviously been stunned by Keith's news, but she wasn't sure where exactly his anger came from. Was it because he hadn't known, because he didn't want his mom replaced or because he was so anti-marriage in general? It was probably a combination of the three, but she didn't want him blowing up at his father.

Keith Ames had always been a bit of a revelation to Dahlia. He was so incredibly different from her own father. Where Casper Windham had been cold and demanding, pushing his children to win at all costs, Mr. Ames had been quietly supportive of Rawlston, encouraging him to find his passion and supporting whatever his son chose to do. Not in a screaming-from-the-sideline way, but in a gently encouraging, do-your-best way.

As a teen, she'd been envious of Rawlston because of his father, and because he was an only child. Her dad not only wanted his children to win, he wanted them to compete with each *other*. No wonder Rawlston seemed to do so well all the time—he was the solo, golden child in his home, and both parents adored him unconditionally.

Dahlia could hear angry, raised voices coming from down the hall. She wasn't close enough to overhear words and, frankly, she didn't want to be. This was a family matter between the two men. Things got quiet. Then she heard Keith laughing loudly, and then raised voices again before Rawlston stormed out. Dahlia barely had time to duck into the kitchen with the caterers so that he wouldn't see her lurking. She worked her way outside, hoping to bump into him casually, but Rawlston was nowhere to be seen.

She jumped when she felt an abrupt tap on her shoulder ten minutes later. She'd barely turned when a folded piece of paper was slapped into her hand.

"Here," Rawlston growled. "I can't wait to be done with this marriage."

"Wait…" But he was gone as fast as he'd appeared. She opened the paper to see his signature, agreeing to allow the law firm to begin the process of dissolving their marriage. It was what she wanted. So why did she feel like chasing after him?

She didn't, of course. She reminded herself that whatever was going on between Rawlston and Keith Ames was none of her business. And there was Keith now, mingling with his guests with a big smile on his face. So the two hadn't killed each other, and Rawlston's bad behavior hadn't dimmed his father's joy. She wouldn't let it dim hers, either.

When Dahlia opened the gate to the new pasture, a hundred sheep galloped through the opening, looking like bouncy cotton balls against the green grass. With a nudge of her heel, the buckskin mare she was riding stepped forward so Dahlia could reach over to close the gate. The well-trained old mare sidestepped obediently until the gate was closed and latched.

"Good girl, Bunny." Dahlia patted the horse's neck. "Chasing after sheep is a lot easier than chasing racehorses, isn't it?"

Bunny—officially King's Sweet Bun—had been Dahlia's mount when she'd worked at the racetrack near Dallas. The mare had been a calming influence on the young colts and fillies Dahlia worked with as a groom. Of course, they didn't all want to *be* calmed. She and the mare had been bitten and kicked at numerous times in the eight years they'd worked there. But sturdy Bunny had always been unflappable around the high-strung youngsters.

Dahlia figured the move to the Fortune ranch was the equivalent of retirement for the thirteen-year-old mare. She'd use her for the occasional check on the herd, just to keep her in shape, but most of Bunny's time would be spent in the partially covered paddock near the stable. Dahlia's daily mount would be her paint stallion. Unlike Bunny, Rebel wasn't a calming influence on *anyone*, especially sheep, which he seemed to have a particular dislike for.

Maybe the stud thought herding sheep was beneath his dignity as a champion cutting horse—a competition that involved herding and outwitting grown cattle. Then again, Rebel hadn't liked the cows much, either. He was a grumpy soul trapped in a gorgeous black-and-white paint body. That was how Dahlia had come to own him. His last owner had given up on him and labeled him *dangerous* after he'd charged at the man's wife, mouth wide-open, with clear intent to do serious harm.

Dahlia had realized a long time ago that stallions are all about ego. And misbehaving ones were more ego-centric than most. She'd learned to honor that ego rather than try to break it. Tough horses wanted respect, but they also *gave* respect to humans who didn't respond to them with fear or anger. Rebel was only five, and he had a lot to learn, but he'd come to trust Dahlia.

She saw the top of a tall cottonwood tree just visible beyond a rolling hill and trotted Bunny in that direction. The sheep seemed content where they were, barely lifting their heads from the grass as she rode past them. As the tree came fully into sight, she was surprised to see a man and horse near it. The horse was in the shade, but the man was working on a nearby fence line. She thought it might be one of the ranch hands, but when he took his hat off, wiped his brow and turned to face her, she was surprised to see it was Rawlston.

"Good morning, neighbor!" She called out to him. He didn't answer, but he gave a slight nod. Was he still in a mood from his father's party? She looked over at his dark chestnut gelding, standing by the tree. "Will he be okay with company?"

"Malloy? Yeah, he's fine with sharing the shade."

She dismounted and tied the reins loosely to the saddle so Bunny could graze by Malloy. She was glad she hadn't ridden Rebel out here today, as that would never have happened. A mottled black-and-white dog came running over to her.

"Who's this?" She knelt to pet the dog, whose stub of a tail was wagging wildly, making his whole butt wiggle.

"That's Tripp. He's an Australian cattle dog. Fearless little guy." Rawlston smiled down at Dahlia and Tripp. "You're gonna need a herding dog of your own, aren't you?"

"I've been thinking about it, yes." She loved dogs, but she knew nothing about using a herding dog. "I need to learn what to do with one first. I've heard it's a science." She stood.

"I know a border collie breeder outside Houston. Bonnie has raised some champions, and she'll teach you how to use them with the sheep. I'll get you her number. It's just a matter of learning their commands." He made the slightest of hand signals, and Tripp promptly moved to sit at his side. "Herding dogs are hyperintelligent and energetic. They make good companions."

As he leaned over to pet his dog's head, Dahlia couldn't help wondering if that companionship was more important to Rawlston than the work. He had no siblings, and he'd told her in Vegas that he only had a few hired hands on the ranch. He had to be lonely. She checked herself. That wasn't her problem.

She walked to the fence line. "I believe you're on the wrong side of this fence, mister."

He shook his head with a slow smile. "I won't swear to it, but I'm pretty sure that old tree is on the property line, so technically if you're on this side of the tree, *you're* the one trespassing. But you're welcome to do so." He looked past her, his smile fading. "You're bringing your sheep up into this range?"

"Well, it's my range, so…yes, of course I am. Why?"

He gave a slight shrug of one shoulder. "Sheep and

cattle don't mix. They had whole range wars about it in the old days."

"Well, then, I guess it's a good thing you're keeping this fence repaired. My sheep will stay over here, and your cows can—" She looked toward his side of the fence. "Oh, are those Brahmans? I didn't know you raised rodeo bulls!" The big, grayish-blond bovines, with long ears and humped backs, were well-known on the rodeo circuit as some of the toughest bulls to ride.

"I don't raise anything for the rodeo, and I only have two bulls at the moment." He followed her gaze to the distant cattle on his side of the fence. "Those are what we call 'gentle Brahmans.' They've been crossbred with Angus and Herefords to take the attitude out of them. I wouldn't recommend trying to *ride* one, but they're actually as gentle as kittens, despite their size."

"What made you go with Brahmans? My brothers said Black Angus was the way to go for our ranch."

"Angus is a good cow, and the meat is in demand. But I like the Brahmans because they can handle the heat of southern Texas so well. The breed originated in Africa." His smile returned. "And I think they look cool."

"They *are* cool. That's one of the reasons I went with the Texas Merino sheep—they can handle the summer heat." She turned to face him. "Oh, and just FYI… I got an email from the law firm, and they'll be sending us the papers to sign within a couple of days. After that, the annulment only takes a few weeks to process."

She expected him to be thrilled, but his face went blank. "That's what you want?"

Did he really just ask that?

"You're the one who barked at me that you couldn't

JO MCNALLY
77

wait for the marriage to be over. Now it will be, and we can both go back to living our lives."

He slid his hat back on with a sigh. "I'm sorry about my attitude on Sunday. Dad just…stunned me. It was a reminder of all the reasons marriage makes no sense as a concept. People aren't meant to pair up forever. It's not sustainable."

She stared for a moment before responding. "Wow. I thought *I* was the cynical one. Clearly *our* marriage makes no sense, but marriage in general is… Well, it's about making a commitment to a person you love. And long marriages do happen, so it's not impossible."

"It's impossible for me."

She'd heard some vague gossip about his marriage to Lana, but couldn't remember the details—only that the divorce had been ugly.

"It's impossible for *us*, I agree. But this will be just a blip on the screen of our lives, Rawlston. You'll find your someone someday."

Chapter Seven

Her words were meant to be comforting and encouraging. They only left Rawlston feeling numb.

"You sound like my dad," he muttered. "I tried those rose-colored glasses once, and got trampled on, so forgive me if I have no interest in trying again."

"What happened with you and Lana, anyway?" Dahlia's voice was soft. Gentle. But her question cut like a dull knife on a salted wound. He braced against the sting, reminding himself it wasn't her fault for being curious. She wasn't being intentionally hurtful…unlike his first wife.

"I'd already enlisted in the navy when Lana and I got serious." He gestured for Dahlia to follow him into the shade near where their horses grazed. Tripp was already napping there, curled into a ball. "But I guess she hadn't thought through what that meant. She loved me wearing my dress white uniform at the wedding, but she had a fit the first time I deployed. She acted as if I had a choice in where I went or for how long."

Dahlia took a bottle of water from her saddlebag. She offered it to him, but he'd brought his own and dug that out.

"Why *did* you choose the navy? You were always the cowboy-est of cowboys when we were teens."

"That was why. I wanted something totally different. My dad thought it was defiance, but it was more…curiosity. I wanted to visit some of the places we'd learned about in school, and I wanted to see the ocean, so it seemed a great way to do both. And I loved it. I worked in navigation and it was different from anything I'd ever done."

"But Lana wasn't impressed?"

He huffed. "To say the least. Lana wanted to be the center of everything. At the time, I saw her ego as strength, but it was really a weakness of hers. She was only happy when everyone's world revolved around her. And I couldn't do that from the Atlantic Ocean. She told me I 'wasn't present' for her."

"Did she send you a Dear John letter?"

"I wish she had." He saw the surprise on Dahlia's face. "If she'd just ended things, I'd probably be on a ship somewhere today. Instead she begged me to come home, making me think we had a chance to make it work. That was back when I thought marriage vows meant something."

Lana had acted like being in the military was a job he could just quit whenever he'd wanted, but it didn't work that way. "When my time was up, I left the navy and came home to save our marriage. Two months later, she left me for the guy who lived next door to us. His wife was a navy pilot, and apparently Lana and Ted had been keeping each other company whenever we were deployed." He took a long drink of water, hoping to wash the bitterness from his throat. "I lost a friend, my wife *and* a career I'd enjoyed."

"You don't enjoy ranching?"

The question surprised him. "That's what you got from that whole story? I love ranching now. But for a while, I'd had a different dream, and Lana stole that from me."

"I'm sorry about your marriage, of course. It just surprises me to hear you mourning a navy career while we're standing here." She gestured around. The cottonwood tree sat atop a small hill, so they had quite a view of ranges sprawling out around them in greens and browns. He nodded.

"I've gotten over that part of the loss. Ranching's hard work, but rewarding. I have no regrets about the life I have. But marriage? No thanks. Four years later, that wound is still raw."

Which made it even more bizarre that he'd stumbled—no matter *how* drunk—into another marriage in Las Vegas.

Dahlia glanced at her watch. "I should head back before the temperature gets higher. I don't want to stress Bunny too much in the heat." She flashed a quick smile. "I should have those papers soon, and we'll make ending *this* marriage less stressful than your last one."

He stepped up to help her mount the buckskin mare, then remembered who she was. Dahlia was a champion, and didn't need his help with horses.

"I heard you bought that ornery paint stud from Hal Templeton. How's he working out for you?"

"Rebel is slightly less ornery these days, at least with me. But he's still not very social. And oddly enough, he doesn't like sheep."

He laughed at that. "He was bred to be a cattle horse,

not to chase around a bunch of stuffed squeak toys." She started to object, but he raised his hand to stop her. "I'm not making fun of your livestock. I'm just saying what that paint horse probably thinks of them." He patted her mare's shoulder, right next to Dahlia's leg. "I'd like to take a look at him sometime. I've got a bay mare I think would be a good cross with his bloodline." He stepped back with a grin. "Maybe we can make his breeding fee part of the divorce settlement."

"It's an annulment, not a divorce." She corrected him like a schoolmarm. "And I take breeding fees seriously in my stable, so if you're really interested, stop by and we can talk. I might even give you a neighborly discount."

She turned her horse and trotted off down the hill away from him. He caught at the reins of his own trusted horse, Malloy, just in case he got any ideas about following. Dahlia's blond hair was free under her Western hat, fluttering lightly as she neared the bottom of the hill. She sat straight in the saddle, like she was born to be there. She'd been riding and showing horses since she was a kid.

Dahlia was a good person. She deserved a better husband than him, for sure. He frowned. She *definitely* deserved a better husband than Carter Powers. Dahlia was smart, but she didn't seem to see how sleazy the guy was—he'd do just about anything for more money and power. The fact that she was now going by the name *Fortune* probably made her all the more enticing to Carter as a spouse. Would she really say yes if he asked?

He mounted Malloy and headed down the fence line in the opposite direction, to a gate at the base of the long slope. Tripp was trotting along behind him. Dahlia couldn't say yes to Carter if she was still married to Rawlston. As much as he disdained the institution, his dad was right. He could use it in order to protect her. Carter would move on in a hurry once Dahlia rejected him—the guy didn't know how to handle losing.

And as soon as that happened, Rawlston could sign those papers and set them both free. It was an absurd idea, but it might just work.

Dahlia was dreaming about Rawlston when her phone began to ring. She blinked, looking around in consternation until she remembered she lived in a log mansion these days. She'd fallen asleep in the overstuffed easy chair near the fireplace, thinking about her conversation with Rawlston under the cottonwood that morning. That was probably why he'd sauntered into her dreams, holding her close and kissing…

The phone rang again, forcing her to wake up for real and find the damn thing. It had fallen into the cushions. She dug it out and frowned at the screen. What was her brother Ridge calling her about at midnight?

"What's wrong?"

Her brother chuckled softly. "Nice greeting, sis. Sorry to do this, but…can you come over to my horse barn? Livvie's not acting right. I'm worried it could be colic…"

She sat up and reached for her boots. "Have you called the vet?"

Just because she'd worked as an aid for the track veterinarian for a few years didn't mean she was qualified to diagnose anything officially.

"I did, but both vets are all the way out in Billington. There was a barn fire and a bunch of horses were injured in the evacuation. They won't make it to Chatelaine for a couple hours yet, and I know how fast a minor case of colic can go bad." Ridge had lost a prize broodmare to the intestinal condition last year. "I'd really appreciate the help, sis."

She tried to push the horror of a stable fire out of her head. It was every horse owner's worst nightmare. "I'm on my way."

They'd begun using golf carts to get around the ranch. It was their mother's idea—something she'd seen on another ranch in the area. Wendy had bought all six of them new golf carts with headlights, comfortable seating and a small cargo basket in back, where golf clubs would normally go. At first they'd all rolled their eyes behind Mom's back. It was a sweet gesture, but it felt silly.

Until they'd started trying to walk the long roadway to each other's homes, or worse, to the main barns over a mile away. Not an impossible distance to walk, unless you were carrying something or were trying to avoid a hike on a hundred-degree August day. But too short to make driving their cars worth it. Within a few days, they'd embraced the golf carts, and started tricking them out for fun.

Dahlia had found dahlia stickers online in a variety of colors and sizes, and had covered her cart in the flowers. Her name was considered unusual by some, but it was a Windham family name from generations back. While there was no proof, everyone had assumed it had originally been inspired by the large, colorful flowers.

The lights were on in the low stable across from Ridge's home, and she found him inside, walking a dapple gray mare up and down the main aisle. Lonestar Livvie was a three-year-old thoroughbred, and she'd won quite a few races. Ridge had high hopes for her, both on the track and as a future broodmare. He looked up in relief when Dahlia walked in.

"Thanks for coming so fast. I heard something on the intercom, so I walked over to the barn to check it out. That's when I saw Livvie biting at her side and I got nervous." All the barns had cameras or intercoms installed. The ranch staff monitored the main barn cameras, but Dahlia and some of her siblings kept monitors in their homes for their own smaller stables, just so they'd hear if something unusual happened during the night.

Dahlia ran her hand down the mare's neck and stepped close. A horse with stomach colic often had pale gums and lips, and an inward look to their gaze. Dahlia checked her mouth, and Livvie's gums were pink and healthy looking. Her eyes didn't look distressed as much as just nervous, and her pulse was close to normal. Dahlia was relieved to discover that the mare's stomach wasn't bloated, and she didn't react when Dahlia pressed against it in a few spots.

"I don't think this is colic, Ridge." Livvie whipped her head around to bite at her side. "But something's definitely bothering her." Dahlia examined the area Livvie had tried to bite. There was a small, hard lump there. When she tried to look more closely, Livvie's ears went flat back. "It looks like a bug bite or maybe even a—" she pressed against it and the horse tried to bite *her* "—yep, it's a bee sting. Probably burns and itches like crazy, doesn't it, girl?" Livvie wasn't ready to forgive her quite yet, shaking her head and stomping a front hoof in anger. "She doesn't seem allergic, but I need to get the stinger out and see if we can make her feel better. Do you have tweezers and ice packs?"

"In the first aid kit on the wall. How would we know if she's allergic?"

Dahlia went to the first aid kit. "Just like humans, really—swelling, increased pulse, lips and gums turning blue. She doesn't have any of that. She seems more ticked off than sick, but the vet may want her to have a steroid to be safe." She returned to Livvie. "In the meantime, let's hold cold compresses on it to get the swelling and pain down." She held up the tweezers. "Hold her head so I don't get bit while I try to find the stinger and get it out."

She was able to do that fairly quickly, and only had to dodge one sideways kick from Livvie in the process. They were taking turns holding compresses on the bump when they both heard something near the open back door of the barn. It was a soft, mewing sound.

"Did you hear that?" Dahlia asked. "Was that the yearling squealing or...?"

Ridge frowned. "The colt's right here across from Livvie. There aren't any horses in those back stalls. Might be a cat or something. There are a few around."

They dismissed it and returned their attention to the mare, whose mood had definitely improved. She was snatching hay from Ridge's hand and chewing it contentedly.

"I think you can save the veterinarian a midnight drive," Dahlia said. "She looks fine now."

Ridge agreed and put her back into her stall. He was finishing a voicemail to the vet when they heard another sound from the back of the barn. This time the sound was more clear, but it made no sense, because it was definitely the sound of an infant crying. They hurried toward the sound, which was coming from an empty stall Ridge used to store bales of hay. They both came to an abrupt halt at the open door.

There was a woman lying on the floor, her back against the stack of hay bales. On her chest was an infant carrier, and inside that carrier was an unhappy baby crying loudly. The petite brunette wasn't responding to the child's cries. Dahlia rushed forward. The woman was unconscious, with a nasty bump on her forehead.

"She's hurt. Call 9-1-1!" Instead, Ridge knelt at her side, staring at the woman. Dahlia looked over at him. "Ridge, do you know her? You need to call someone."

"Just…wait." Her brother reached out to remove the baby from the carrier, cradling the infant in his arms. "Let's figure out what's going on first. The baby looks healthy. Looks like a girl, with hair just like her mom."

They did both have the same auburn hair, but Dahlia was more of a skeptic than Ridge. "We don't know if this is the baby's mother. Maybe she's a kidnapper or…"

"She's not a kidnapper. Look at her neck, at that birthmark. And look at the baby."

He was right—the woman and child had matching birthmarks, shaped almost like a star, on their necks.

"Okay, maybe she's the mom. But look at her! She needs medical attention, and why is she hiding in your barn? Who's she running from? It could be a custodial battle or—"

"Or maybe she's protecting the baby from someone, Dahlia. You don't know."

"Neither do you!" The baby's cries got louder, and

Dahlia lowered her voice. "This is for the authorities to figure out. This woman needs help. If you're not going to call, then I will." She pulled her phone from her back pocket, but Ridge put his hand on hers, stopping her.

"She has a bump on the head, but the bleeding has already stopped. I've got a friend I can call." He looked straight into Dahlia's eyes to make his case. "A *doctor* friend who lives in Chatelaine Hills. I know Mitch will come over. If he thinks she needs a hospital, then we'll take her. She ended up in my barn for a reason, and I'm not going to put her at risk of being found until I know for sure who's after her."

Ridge was the baby of the family, and tended to be pretty lighthearted in his approach to life. He also had a reputation as a bit of a playboy. But she'd never known him to be this impractical or impulsive. Not that he wasn't a loving brother and a good man, but watching him bouncing an infant in his arms and arguing for *not* calling the police to handle this situation was a bit of an out-of-body experience for Dahlia. Against every instinct she had, she felt compelled to support him. At least for the moment.

"Maybe there's something in the baby bag." It was a small bag, but she was relieved to find a baby bottle in there with milk in it, a small container of formula, diapers, and a few items of clothing. But nothing that would identify the mother.

"Look!" Ridge said. "On the flap of the bag." He tugged at the flap of the pink-and-white-gingham bag. There was a name embroidered there in minty green thread. *Evie.*

"Well, I think it's safe to say that's the baby's name.

I'm guessing little Evie is around three months old."
Dahlia held the mother's wrist, checking her pulse. It
was strong and steady. Her breathing was steady, too.
She lifted her eyelids and checked her eyes—they also
seemed fine. "The woman doesn't seem to have any
other injuries than the bump on her head. But, Ridge—"

"I'll call Mitch right now to come check her out. And I
promise I'll follow whatever medical advice he gives me."
The baby was quiet, content in the warmth of his arms.
He was staring down at the little girl. His expression was
soft...sweetly intimate in a way that made Dahlia smile.
He looked up. "I just can't shake the idea that they might
be in more danger if we report this to the police. Not *from*
the police, but from whomever she's running from. If they
know where she is, they might try to take this baby from
her, or...worse." He looked up at Dahlia. "I can't take that
chance. Not until I know."

"It's a huge risk, Ridge. You're taking responsibility
for them both."

"Trust me, sis. Please."

She'd never known her brother to beg. She let out a
long sigh. "Okay. But I'm not leaving until I see you call
this doctor friend of yours."

Dahlia called Ridge first thing in the morning. He
assured her that not only were his surprise houseguests
still there, but they were both awake and doing fine. In
fact, the mother had woken while his doctor pal was
there last night. Her head wound only required a couple
of stitches, but there was one big problem. She claimed
not to know her own name or who she was. Ridge tried to

explain it away as something his doctor friend said was probably temporary amnesia, but Dahlia had her doubts.

"Don't you think it's a little convenient that she can't give you her name?"

"Look, even if she *does* know her name, I can't blame her for being cautious about sharing it." He huffed out a breath. "Like I said last night, I'm convinced she's hiding from someone or something."

"Does she remember Evie?"

"Yes. As soon as she saw her, she knew the baby's name and knew she was her child. She's very protective of her. She told me this morning that she knows they're in danger, but she doesn't know why or who the threat is."

"So, where is she going to go?" Dahlia asked.

"They'll stay with me for now. They'll be safe here while she works on getting her memory back."

"Ridge, you can't just take them in like that."

"Well, I just did. I named her Hope."

"*Excuse* me?"

"The woman. I have to call her something, so I've named her Hope." He paused. "I'll protect her, Dahlia."

"Yes, I'm sure you will. But who will protect *you*? Be careful, Ridge."

He promised he would be, but she couldn't help thinking it was too late for that. She'd promised to trust his decision, so she hoped for the best. But she also promised herself she'd keep an eye on all of them.

She'd been scrolling through her emails on her laptop as they talked, and she opened one from the Nevada law firm as soon as they hung up. Attached to the email were annulment papers. She sat back and smiled. All she had to do was sign them, get Rawlston's signature, and their so-called marriage would be over.

Ridge's problems might just be beginning, but hers were about to be over.

Chapter Eight

Rawlston read Dahlia's text again, after finishing his first morning coffee and starting on his second.

Papers attached. Sign and return them and we'll be single again. Yay!

There was an attachment to the text. All he had to do was send it to his printer, sign it and get it to Dahlia for her signature. He'd be free of marriage. She'd be free *to* marry. To marry Carter Powers. He scowled at the phone. Carter would only use Dahlia—her beauty, her name, her money—to advance his own agenda. Rawlston had heard rumblings that the guy was looking at a run for political office.

She couldn't say yes to Carter as long as she was wed to Rawlston. The thought kept rolling over and over in his head. It would mean telling lies. Little ones, perhaps, but a lot of them. To Dahlia. And it would mean staying legally married, at least for a while. That would be wrong.

But if he was doing it to *protect* Dahlia…wouldn't that be a noble cause? Would it be worth a few little white lies to keep her from walking into a disaster with Carter? It wasn't like he'd be trapping her—or himself—in marriage forever. Carter had a short attention span, and he'd need a partner before his campaign started. As soon as Dahlia said no, the jerk would be on the hunt for someone else. And *then* Rawlston would sign those damn papers and set them both free. He was only talking about another month or two.

Rawlston took a sip of his coffee, surprised that he was seriously thinking about this.

He couldn't tell Dahlia he *wanted* to stay married. She'd get the wrong idea and it would backfire. After all, she didn't want to have a relationship with him now, any more than she had back in school. He wasn't looking to court the woman anyway. So he'd have to just… stall her for a while. Similar to riding a good cutting horse in competition, whenever she tried to break past him, he'd have to move fast to hold her in place. Metaphorically, of course. He was *helping* her, not keeping her as a hostage.

Oh, damn. This was actually becoming a plan. One he couldn't tell anyone about. He set his coffee mug down and picked up the phone, tapping a response.

Printer's on the blink. I'll have to go to town but can't til tomorrow earliest.

He winced as he hit Send. It was a tiny fib, but still. There was a pause before he saw she was typing.

My printer works. You wanted to see Rebel up close, so come to the ranch later and I'll have the papers ready.

Rawlston scrubbed a hand down his face, mulling it over. He really was interested in seeing that stallion. And also had been wanting to see the Fortune Family Ranch. He sighed. This plan was going to be more challenging than he'd thought. But he had to find a way to hold her off a little bit longer.

Can't today. Tomorrow afternoon?

That would give him time to decide if any of this was a good idea. Her response was quick.

Fine. Anytime after 3 works.

Rawlston was impressed with the Fortunes' ranch. It was hard *not* to be, with thirty-five hundred acres of prime range land, multiple barns and *six* big log homes on the north shore of Lake Chatelaine. That was in addition to the large main house, where Wendy Fortune lived. She'd also inherited an actual castle from her grandfather, Wendell Fortune. Rawlston had heard Wendy was busy converting the castle into a boutique hotel and event venue.

Each of the housing lots on the ranch was spacious, with a long driveway leading off from the main road. The log houses were similar, but still unique. They didn't look like cookie-cutter homes—each had some feature or roof angle that the others didn't. Dahlia told him her home was the last one at the end of the road.

As he continued driving, he realized that, just like her rangeland, the lot where her contemporary log home stood bordered his land. They were technically next-door neighbors, even if his house was another mile or so over the gently rolling hills, and away from the lakeshore.

Dahlia's home wasn't massive, but it was a lot of house for one person. The center looked like an A-frame, with single-story wings extending out to the sides. Large windows went up to the peak, giving the impression you could look right through the house to the lake. He didn't turn into her driveway, though. Instead, he went to the barns across from her house. There was a golf cart parked there covered with dahlia stickers, so he assumed it was hers.

The stable had a narrow loft above the main level, and the sheep barn behind it was one-story. Both had horizontal panels under the roofline that were raised up and fastened to allow air to move through. The stable had doors that opened from each stall into small, individual paddocks which were partially shaded. It was a nice setup for the horses, allowing them more space to move while sheltering them from the blistering mid-August sun.

The sheep barn looked like it was mostly open—more of a shelter than a barn, since sheep were generally out to graze, unless they were ill or the weather turned nasty. Dahlia walked out of that sheep barn and seemed surprised to see him getting out of his truck. She took off her leather work gloves and gave him a smile that made his heart skip a beat.

"Oh, hi. I was just tossing some feed to a couple of moms and their lambs. I'll be weaning them soon. Give me a minute to switch gears to horses, okay?" She gestured to the stable. "Rebel's in the back corner stall. Be careful—he's not crazy about men, for good reason. He was abused as a colt. He still likes to bite once in a while, but most of the time he's bluffing."

Rawlston understood what she meant when he got to the stall. The big paint horse was built like a Mack truck, with a long mane that whipped when he shook his head menacingly. He blew out a sharp snort and stomped a front hoof, then made a short charge at the opened top of the stall door. Rawlston stepped back, for his own protection and to appear less threatening to the stallion.

"Easy, big guy." He kept his voice low and steady. "I'm thinking of bringing you a girlfriend, so play nice."

"He *is* nice." Dahlia walked to Rawlston's side. "He just likes to test people he doesn't know."

"Looks like you have your hands full with him, but someone told me you were a 'stallion whisperer.'"

She chuckled. "That all started at the racetrack. There was a three-year-old colt who was an absolute menace to the trainers, grooms and jockeys. Everyone tried to subdue him, but he wasn't the rogue they labeled him as. He was just smart and bored, which made him mischievous. I started giving him different stall toys to play with and we upped his exercise time to burn off some of that excess energy. I showed him he wasn't scaring me. He eventually settled down, and people started calling me to help with *their* rambunctious colts." She shrugged. "And a reputation was born."

"And what about Rebel here? Is he just being playful?" Rawlson asked.

"No, Rebel's being defensive. That makes him a little more dangerous. He was abused—not by Hal, but on the ranch where he was born. Then Hal and his stable hands treated him like a killer stallion, so Rebel's never learned how to relax and behave properly. He's great in competition, but in the barn, he thinks everyone's out to get him. Isn't that right, pretty boy?"

Dahlia walked confidently to the stall door. Rebel shook his head and snorted, then showed his teeth in a mock bite attempt. But she calmly talked to him and ran her fingers down his face. He lowered his head, still tense, but giving her access to the top of his head. She started scratching behind his ear and the horse began to settle. He brought his head over the half door and bumped Dahlia affectionately. His mouth began moving in a chewing motion, which signaled he was relaxed and trusting. She slid a halter over his head, snapped on a lead and brought him out of the stall. "Do you want me to saddle him up, or do you want to see him move free in the round paddock?"

"Moving free is fine—no need to go through a lot of fuss. I can already see how impressive he is," he replied.

It was no exaggeration. The horse was drop-dead gorgeous. Close to sixteen hands tall, broad chested and muscular, with a striking black-and-white coat. His conformation was near perfect, and his head was refined— not too long, broad between the eyes and sculptured. Rawlston knew without seeing the horse move that he'd be a great cross with his mare in the spring.

Dahlia led Rebel out the barn door and to the sturdy round pen. The posts were like telephone poles, and the wooden rails were tall enough to contain a stallion who might have a wandering eye. It was larger than most training pens, probably seventy feet across. Rebel started prancing as they neared the gate, but he never pulled on the lead in Dahlia's hand. The stallion was high-spirited, but well-mannered. It was an attractive combination.

The dynamic between horse and woman was pretty damn attractive, too. Dahlia might *look* Hollywood, but she was a genuine horsewoman through and through. Rawlston had a hard time taking his eyes off of her.

When Dahlia latched the gate and unfastened the lead, Rebel let out a loud snort and charged away from her, head and tail high. Dahlia joined Rawlston, sitting on the top rail to watch. He had to remind himself that he was there to see the *horse*.

"I can see why they named him Rebel," he remarked. One of the horse's black patches covered both eyes, like a mask.

"Yes," she nodded. "I imagine it was really cute when he was a foal. His full name is Mendelsohn's Rebellious Heart. He came from the Mendelsohn ranch up in Oklahoma. That's where he was handled so badly." She turned to face him. "Oh, hey—don't let me forget that I have those annulment papers in the barn."

He kept his face carefully neutral. He'd been hoping she *would* forget, and he had no intention of reminding her. He asked about Rebel's pedigree, hoping horse talk would distract her.

Dahlia slapped her computer shut with a muttered curse.

"Whoa," Sabrina laughed from the kitchen. "What did that laptop ever do to you?"

"It's not the laptop, it's the email I just read from Rawlston Ames." The man was beginning to get on her very last nerve. "He has more excuses than the Gulf of Mexico has water!"

"Excuses about what?" Her twin came into the great room and handed her a glass of wine. "Arlo said he heard Rawlston might be breeding one of his mares to your Rebel. Is he trying not to pay for it or something?" Sabrina sat. "Oh, is this about the annulment?"

"Yes! He's making me crazy! I texted him the papers and he said his printer was broken. He came to the stables to see Rebel at the beginning of the week, and I had the physical papers ready to sign, and get this—" she stared up at the ceiling "—he told me he'd forgotten his *special pen*. Can you believe it?" She stared at Sabrina. "Apparently, he uses a special lucky pen his grandfather gave him to sign important documents, and he didn't have it with him. He refused to sign them without it!"

"Well, people can be superstitious about things like that," Sabrina said with a slight shrug.

"But I *told* him I'd have the paperwork, so he knew I wanted him to sign them. Why wouldn't he bring his damn lucky pen? And now he just emailed me saying he can't find the papers. He *lost* them."

"Sis, I know you're in a hurry to put this marriage in your rearview mirror, but it's clearly not a priority for Rawlston." She added gently, "That doesn't mean he's plotting against you. It just means he's not feeling as urgent about it as you are. You're living your own lives as if nothing happened, so the marriage isn't affecting him one way or the other."

"That's nice for *him*, but I need to get this done before Carter gets back."

"Ah, yes. Good old Carter. Are you missing him yet?"

"What kind of question is that?" Dahlia huffed. "Of course I miss him…"

When she thought of him. Which admittedly wasn't as much as she probably should. But she blamed that on the stress of this damn Vegas wedding. She took a sip of wine, then told Sabrina that Carter texted her nearly every day, which was a slight exaggeration. Carter seemed so absorbed in this business trip—the exact nature of that business wasn't clear to her—that he'd only reached out once or twice a week.

"Oh, wow." Sabrina rolled her eyes. "How romantic."

"It's *attentive.* And he called just last night."

She didn't elaborate on how well, or *not* well, that conversation had gone. She knew her twin's dislike for Carter, and directed the conversation back to knitting patterns and preferred types of wool.

After Sabrina headed back to her own house, Dahlia refilled her coffee mug and went outside to the deck. Sabrina had insisted from the start that Carter was "just like Dad." Craving power and success at any cost. Dahlia had seen some of those things, of course, but that was just part of being a businessman.

Yes, Carter was a little secretive about the details of his work in finance. And he'd done it in a way that made her feel patronized, as if she wouldn't understand his big, complicated world. But he'd insisted that she was his shelter from talking about all of that. Busy with her move to Chatelaine, she'd let it slide.

She'd heard rumors about his integrity, but trash talking was just part of being in business. Her father had dealt with all of that, too. Her coffee mug stopped halfway to her lips. Which meant Carter really *was* like

Dad. And most of the rumors about Dad's ruthlessness in business had been true. What if the rumors about Carter were, too?

She shook off her doubts and headed to the barns to check on a few ewes and lambs she'd brought indoors because they'd seemed stressed. Between the stifling heat last week and being moved from their original home in the Texas panhandle to the Chatelaine ranch, some of the ewes with the youngest lambs had lost some weight, so she wanted to give them good alfalfa hay to build them back up again before rejoining the herd. The heat wave had eased now, and they all seemed rested and content this morning. She figured they could go back out to the range by tomorrow.

And speaking of the herd and the range—she hadn't seen the herd since yesterday morning, and even then, they were nearly out of sight on one of the farthest little hills. They had thirty-five hundred acres to roam, but she figured she'd better go check on them, just to be sure all was well. It would be a good excuse to give Rebel a ride and burn off some of his perpetual energy.

The Fortune ranch was feeling more like home every day. The main barns and office were up and running, keeping her siblings busy. Nash was the ranch foreman, Arlo was the overall planner and manager, Sabrina was keeping the books, and Jade wanted to open a petting zoo of some kind. Ridge was working his way through all the jobs on the ranch, learning the ropes. Dahlia was making plans to sell wool and woolen arts and crafts by the holidays. Next spring she'd be bringing in shearers to harvest the wool from her very own sheep, and then her business plans would really be rolling. Which brought her thoughts back to Carter as she saddled Rebel.

Last night's call had been unsettling. Carter was in Italy this week, and sounded like he'd had too much espresso—he was talking a mile a minute, without giving her much opportunity to respond. His trip was going well, he was setting up business connections, but more importantly, *political* connections. Apparently he was getting support from "very important people," whatever that meant. He was excited, so she was happy for him.

At least, she *had* been until he made an offhand comment that they could be living in Austin soon. That was hours away. She reminded him that she was just getting settled in Chatelaine, and Carter had laughed. He'd *laughed*.

"Don't get me wrong, Bo Peep—the ranch, the sheep and all of that is cute, but come on, you don't really expect us to *live* on your family's ranch, do you?"

He had a point—Carter was no rancher. It was odd… she hadn't once pictured Carter in her home. Or on the ranch at all. Rawlston had walked into her stables to see Rebel with an ease that Carter would never have. Carter didn't even like to ride.

It seemed she and Carter had a lot to work out before she thought about accepting a ring from him. But she had to deal with this pesky marriage to Rawlston first.

She led the stallion out of the barn and mounted, spending a moment settling his prancing down to a more sedate walk before she tried to tackle opening a gate from the saddle. It took a few tries, but she finally got Rebel through it, then managed to latch it. Afterward, he was as ready for a good run as she was, but she kept him working between a walk and trot for the first part of the ride.

He didn't like it, but Dahlia gave him just enough leeway to get out his friskiness without disobeying her commands. The big horse started to settle after a few minutes. He was paying attention to her leg cues now, and his head dropped as he relaxed. Eventually he stopped tugging on the reins. The sun was hidden behind clouds at the moment, making it more comfortable for riding.

She located the sheep herd near the tall cottonwood tree by the fence line. And just like the last time she'd been there, Rawlston was working on the fence line. She let Rebel have a gallop up the hill, scattering the sheep along the way. By the time she reined him in as they reached the tree, the horse was snorting and prancing, ears back at the sight of Rawlston's horse grazing. The chestnut was unconcerned and unimpressed.

Rawlston stood, his hands on his hips. He looked... annoyed. That was an emotion she didn't often see on his face. Not only did he *look* something like Matthew McConaughey with his light brown hair and lanky appearance, but his *attitude* was a lot like McConaughey's, too. Laid-back and always seeming vaguely amused, as if he might break out with an "alright, alright, alright" of his own. But right now he did not look chill at all. She wondered if he was angry about her riding Rebel up here, but his horse didn't seem to care.

"You looking for your sheep?" he asked sharply.

"Well, yeah. But I found them back there. What's—"

"You didn't find all of 'em."

"What are you talking about?" She didn't like his accusing tone, especially when she had no idea what she was being accused of.

"Take a look. Tripp's rounding up the last of 'em now." He gestured across the fence line toward his property. She could see a dozen or more cream-colored Brahmans grazing. And... *Oh, no.* There were at least six of her sheep with the cattle. The small dog was skulking around behind the sheep, moving them away from the cattle, who were ignoring the drama.

"How on earth did they get over there? Was the fence down?"

Rawlston grabbed the lower line of barbed wire and pulled it up, pointing to the tufts of white wool attached to it. "The fence is just fine. For *cattle*. But your sheep have discovered they can get *under* it, and onto my range."

She dismounted, tucking Rebel's reins through her belt loop. One tug and he'd pull free, but she'd been training him to stay close. She didn't dare let him graze freely—he wasn't *that* well trained. She inspected the fence, her heart dropping.

"Damn, that's a lot of wool. Your fence is shearing my sheep!"

"My fence is..." Rawlston stared at her. "Your sheep are grazing on *my* land!"

"Oh, calm down. They're sheep, not vacuum cleaners. I don't think your precious cows will starve because a few sheep spent a little time over there."

"Dahlia, Tripp's already brought a dozen or more of your little darlings back where they belong. These are the last of them." The dog expertly nipped at the heels of the protesting sheep, who hurried under the wire Rawlston was holding up for them. "This is a serious problem. Sheep don't eat the same way cows do. Sheep yank grass up by the roots, and they can ruin grazing for cattle."

She tugged at the large clumps of wool hanging from the fence, ignoring Rawlston's glare. She tucked the wool into her pocket. "Nonsense. If sheep pulled grass up by the roots, I wouldn't have any pasture left."

He followed her gesture to the range behind her, which still had plenty of green grass. Then he shook his head sharply. "Maybe you still have pasture because they're over here eating *my* grass."

"You're being ridiculous." She folded her arms on her chest. Lord save her from impossible men this week!

"Really? I told you before that entire range wars were fought over sheep and cattle competing for the same grazing land." He took a beat, and his shoulders eased. "Look, I'm not saying they've destroyed my pastures today. I was up here two days ago and the fence was wool-free. But we do have to solve this." He seemed to notice Rebel for the first time. "You brought the stallion. I thought he hated sheep?"

She looked over her shoulder at her horse. "Did you see how flat his ears were when the sheep trotted by? He's not a fan, but he knows he'd better behave when I have the reins."

"And you think your belt loop will stop him if he doesn't?"

"I told you he's not the killer horse everyone made him out to be." She reached out and scratched Rebel's neck. He nudged his head against her.

Rawlston's eyes softened. "Because of you."

She hesitated, then nodded. She'd never been a fan of

false modesty. "I suppose so, yes. So what do you think we should do about my wandering sheep?" She smiled at his dog, now sitting attentively at his side. "Other than employ Tripp on a daily basis."

"Tripp and I can't be running this fence line every day—I have a thousand other acres to tend. Besides, he's a cattle dog, not a sheep dog."

Rawlston seemed especially testy this morning.

"Is there something else bothering you?"

He rubbed the back of his neck and sighed, staring at the ground.

"It's my father."

Alarmed, Dahlia reached out to hold his arm. "Keith? Is he okay?"

"Physically? Fine." He scowled. "Mentally? I'm honestly not sure. I met his so-called fiancée, JoAnn, last night. They're getting married next week, and the whole thing is just absurd!"

Chapter Nine

Rawlston tried to hang on to his rising temper. He'd been agitated—no, more like *furious*—all morning. He'd woken up this way, after a fitful night of dreams that bounced between his mother and Dahlia and stupid weddings. His mother, being replaced by JoAnn marrying his father. Dahlia, being kept from marriage because she'd married *him*.

"Rawlston?" Dahlia's voice was low and soft, snapping him back to the present. They were standing on the hill between their properties. His gelding was nearby, grazing quietly. Rebel was on alert behind Dahlia, nostrils flared and ears up, but standing still.

And Dahlia was staring up at him, concern clear in her blue eyes. The sun was coming out from behind the clouds, so he nodded toward the cottonwood tree. "Let's go in the shade. Will your horse be okay with Malloy nearby?"

She began walking toward the tree. "He'll be fine. Rebel likes the ladies, hates other studs, but pretty much ignores geldings." Sure enough, the stallion followed her quietly. His reins were just pulled through a belt loop on her jeans, but he acted as if he was tied to her. Enthralled with her. Enchanted by her.

Or maybe that was just Rawlston.

"Don't get me wrong—I want Dad to be happy. But this marriage is a mistake on so many levels." He just couldn't figure out how to stop it.

"What's she like?" Dahlia asked.

"She's…different. She's nice enough, but—"

Dahlia pursed her lips in thought, tipping her head to the side. "But she's not your mom?"

He got Dahlia's point, but he disagreed. "I don't expect her to *be* my mom. I'm not clinging to Mom's memory and thinking no one can live up to her or anything like that." That might not be true deep down but he was certainly not gonna admit it. "I'm all for Dad finding someone. But JoAnn is this sturdy New England farm woman."

"I don't know what that means." Dahlia pulled up a handful of grass and fed it to Rebel.

"She's…" He couldn't figure out how to describe his father's wife-to-be. "If you remember my mom, she was quiet and…dignified. She did charity work and served on the library board. She was afraid of horses, so she took care of the house while Dad handled the ranch work."

Dahlia nodded. "Your mom always looked so classy and put-together, even at horse shows. Dressed to the nines and never a hair out of place. She wasn't a snob, though," she rushed to say. "She was sweet. I never realized she was afraid of horses, but now that you've mentioned it, she *did* stay up in the stands when we were in the ring. But…you keep describing your mom when I'm asking about JoAnn."

"Take everything I just said about Mom and flip to its opposite, and that's JoAnn. She's loud and outgoing. She's already been out in the barn cleaning stalls and she and Dad went riding yesterday. She's also making plans to double the size of the vegetable garden, and said she'll build the raised beds herself." His mouth turned downward. "JoAnn's got a very…casual…style. She was wearing this long denim skirt and her hair was in braids." He stopped, hearing his words and cringing a bit. "And all of that sounds superficial, doesn't it?"

Dahlia raised one shoulder. "Pretty much, yeah. You can't hold it against her that she's not your mom—that's not her fault."

"It's not about what that means to me as much as what it means for my dad. Why would he fall for someone so completely different? It's like he intentionally sought out Mom's opposite, and now he wants to *marry* her. They have nothing in common!"

"Actually, it sounds like they have a *lot* in common. She rides, she works outside, she's outgoing like he is…" Her words slowed to silence. "And you don't want me debating this, do you?"

He didn't. But damn if she wasn't right on all counts. "I want you to agree with everything I'm saying. But I think I *need* to hear your viewpoint." He sighed heavily. "Does it mean he and my mom *weren't* suited for each other? He always said she made him complete, like a piece he didn't know was missing until he met her."

Dahlia leaned her back against the tree and removed her Western hat to wipe her brow. The sun's reappearance after last night's rain had caused the temperature and humidity to start climbing again. Rawlston went to his saddlebag and pulled out a couple bottles of water, handing her one.

"Your mom and dad were terrific together," she assured him after she took a sip. "They looked at each other with a love I never saw between my own parents. They really were a perfect fit. But…" She looked up at him with a soft smile. "Puzzle pieces have more than one side. They can fit perfectly together with more than one piece. JoAnn fits differently with your dad, but that doesn't mean they're not right for each other. My advice is to trust your father's judgment on this."

That was going to be easier said than done, even if he suspected Dahlia was right.

"I'll try." He opened his water and took a swig. "Marriage just seems like a drastic step."

After a pause, Dahlia gave him a pointed look. "Speaking of marriage, we really do need to get those papers signed. I texted you a pdf file yesterday for you to print and sign. I texted the same file two days ago. And I emailed it to you two days before that." She sighed, and he braced himself to hear all about Carter again. She watched Malloy snatch at some tall grass at the base of the tree. "I don't like lying to everyone."

No mention of Carter? *Interesting.*

"My internet's been screwy lately, but I'll check when I get home."

They both knew he was lying. Usually, this was where Dahlia got mad. Instead, she rolled her eyes and opened her water bottle.

"Yeah, I bet you will. God, it's getting hot again." She took a gulp of water and stared at the bottle for a moment. Then she dumped all the water over her head, letting it run down her face and neck, soaking the pale yellow knit top she wore. "That's better."

The water made her top transparent, along with the

lacy bra beneath it. Rawlston knew he should probably look away, but he was a hot-blooded man. And he was her husband. She caught his expression, then glanced down at her chest.

"Dude, you saw me naked in Vegas. This shouldn't shock you all that much."

"Trust me," he said, doing his best to keep his gaze on her eyes. "That is a sight I'll never forget. When I woke up to you wrapped around me, nothing but bare skin... You were—you *are*—beautiful."

Her lips parted in surprise at the compliment. Something shifted in her posture. She seemed to let her guard down a bit, and her voice softened.

"Is that why you won't sign the annulment papers? You want another night together?"

"Why? Are you offering?" His body responded immediately to the thought of making love to Dahlia again.

"Of course not." A pause. "Unless it will help me get your signature. I'd have to at least think about it if that were the case, but I'd lose all respect for you in the process."

That night with Dahlia had been all he'd thought about since leaving Las Vegas. But bartering for sex was wrong on every level. He stepped closer to her. She pressed back against the tree, but her eyes never left his. It was almost as if she was daring him to do this. To kiss her. Was she *hoping* he would?

"I'd never use sex like that, Dolly." Rawlston pushed a strand of her hair behind her ear, then left his fingertips brushing against her neck. He could see her pulse beneath the thin skin there. "But I may just kiss you. Just enough to remind myself how sweet you taste." His head dropped close to hers, and their noses brushed against each other. "Would that be okay? If I kissed you?"

She placed one hand over his heart, and he figured she was holding him off. Pushing him away. Instead, she twisted her fingers into his shirt and tugged him closer. Bringing him near enough for her to stand on her tiptoes and touch her mouth to his.

Yes, please.

His arms slid around her waist, his hands gliding up her spine. Was this really happening? Her lips pressed on his and his mind stopped analyzing. He only cared about sensation now, not thoughts. Not doubts. He returned the kiss, his tongue pushing past her willing lips to taste her. It was as if he'd been struck by lightning. Every moment of their wedding night came back to him—every kiss, every touch, every orgasm. They'd been amazing together, and it felt amazing now as her arms wrapped around his neck. Their heads turned, seeking better access to each other. She lifted her chin, exposing her long neck, and he traced kisses and nibbles all the way to her shoulder.

He didn't want to stop, but they were outdoors, with two horses, a few dozen cattle and a hundred sheep watching them. Rawlston pulled back, but her fingers tangled in his hair, preventing him from getting away. With a muttered curse, his mouth covered hers again. Let all those watching eyes be damned. He wasn't going to stop until she did.

His beautiful wife.

Dahlia had no idea what she was doing, or why. And *she* was the one who'd started this. Sure, it was Rawlston's idea, but he wouldn't have pressed it if she hadn't kissed him. Once their lips connected, it was all over for both of them.

He kissed a trail down her neck, interspersed with nips of his teeth on her skin. Her body was on fire, raging with desire. She was surprised the tall grass around them hadn't burst into flames by now. Rawlston hesitated, but she held him close, gripping his hair. She needed this. She wasn't sure why, but she needed his embrace. Needed his kiss. Needed *him*.

He drew back again, staring down into her eyes, looking as dazed as she felt. With the slight bit of space between them, the heat cooled enough for her to think more clearly. And she definitely should *not* be jumping Rawlston's bones like this. Bad idea. Big mistake. Not the way to end their marriage. She straightened, and he stepped away, respecting her space. Of course. Always the gentleman.

He cleared his throat sharply. "We probably shouldn't—"

She huffed out a laugh. "We *definitely* shouldn't. I'm not sure what just happened, but let's…forget it, okay?"

One corner of his mouth lifted in amusement. "You think I'm going to forget that? I'm betting you won't, either. But we can agree not to do it again. I was agitated about my dad and—"

"Please tell me you didn't kiss me because of your father."

"I'm pretty sure *you* kissed *me*, madam."

"That's true. Sorry." She turned away, pretending to check the horses, who were both just fine.

"Don't be sorry," he said thickly. "It was exactly what I needed, along with your commonsense advice, of course."

"Advice and a kiss. More than you'd get from Beau Weatherly at the coffee shop. Think I should set up my own table there?" She was feeling almost giddy, as if that kiss gave her a shot of adrenaline.

Rawlston took her arm, turning her to face him. "Don't go giving those kisses away, Dahlia Fortune."

Still feeling playful, she patted his hand. "Why? Do you want them all?"

He started to answer. She could swear he started to say *yes*. But he caught himself, clamping his lips together and moving away from her. There was a sudden thread of seriousness to the conversation. *Did* he want all her kisses? Did he want all of *her*? She couldn't decide how that made her feel. Why was her heart racing?

And just like that, things turned awkward. Her amusement flipped to irritation, probably because she had no idea what was happening between them. She gathered Rebel's reins and put her foot in the stirrup, swinging up into the saddle.

"I should get back before it gets any hotter."

A spark of humor shone in Rawlston's eyes, picking up on the unintended double meaning. "Wise decision. But we haven't decided who's going to pay for fixing the sheep problem. I'm going to have to add a lower strand of wire to keep them off my land."

"You made a point of telling me the fence is on your land, so my guess is you'll pay for it."

"But they're *your* sheep."

She looked down the hill to the herd of fluffy sheep grazing her land. "Maybe it was a one-time trespass." She met his gaze. Darn…she'd done it again. Her cheeks heated.

"Maybe." Rawlston nodded, pretending to be considering the idea. "But maybe it'll happen more than once."

"It won't." She slapped the reins on Rebel's neck, turning him for home. "I'll make sure of it."

Dahlia stabbed at the muslin stretched on a large embroidery frame. Sometimes she thought the main reason she enjoyed wool art was that it involved stabbing. Lots and lots of stabbing. She reminded herself to pay attention. The special felting needles were not only incredibly sharp, but they were also barbed. When stabbed into a ball of loose, raw wool, each motion in and out created knots in the wool fibers. Eventually the loose wool would be tightened into a firm shape, guided with her hands. In this case, she was creating the trunk of a tree. She'd already formed dozens of tiny leaves in fall colors that would become part of the three-dimensional scene she was creating on the muslin.

Her siblings were talking about opening a small shop near the office, featuring ranch products, and she and Sabrina had offered to showcase their art there. Dahlia's needle felting had started with her creating cute little animals and ornaments ten years ago. Then she went to a wool show and discovered people were creating beautiful scenes on stretched muslin, with swirls of colored wool and the occasional three-dimensional accent. It felt freeing to start something without a specific pattern to follow. She couldn't do it "wrong" if it was freeform.

Dahlia knew that was a holdover from growing up with Casper Windham as a father. Everything had to be the best, the winningest, the most perfect. It was a pressure that she'd never handled well. She'd honed her competitiveness while showing horses and doing rodeos, and her father had always been happy when she came home with blue ribbons. Anything *less* than a blue ribbon would earn her a lecture on trying harder. Coming in second out of fifty competitors was *losing* in Dad's eyes.

Creating art, where there was no *right* or *wrong* was something that just didn't compute in her father's mind. What was the point of sculpting a dog out of wool if it wasn't a photo-quality likeness of the actual dog? Or if it couldn't be sold for lots of money? Making the effort for the "fun of it" was pointless to him, which made her more determined to do things like be a groom at the track rather than own the horses and make the money. Or why she'd rather raise her own sheep in order to create her own wool for her personal artwork.

And yet… She'd never quite succeeded in quieting her father's voice in her head, whispering that whatever she was doing wasn't good enough.

Her mobile phone rang at her side, snapping her out of her own head and making her jump just enough that she managed to stab her finger. She was still cursing as she swiped the phone, not bothering to look at the screen.

"Is this a bad time?" Rawlston was laughing on the other end of the call.

"No, I just stabbed myself."

His laughter was gone in an instant. "Are you okay?"

"It's just a needle poke. I'll live." She checked the time—it was almost 9 p.m. "Why are you calling?"

"I just… I wanted to apologize for this morning."

"Which part? Having a hissy fit about my sheep or kissing me?"

"I was thinking more of the part where I dumped

all my feelings about my dad and JoAnn on you." He paused. "Do I need to apologize for the kiss?"

"No. I kissed you, remember? And you don't need to apologize for talking about your dad, either." She glanced at the kitchen island and saw a folder sitting there. "But if you feel like making amends, you could stop by and sign the annulment papers."

There was a *long* pause this time. Finally, he just said "Tomorrow night?"

She felt an odd little thrill at the idea of Rawlston coming to her house. At night. To talk over dinner and wine. She gave herself a mental shake. There was a purpose to this meeting.

"Six o'clock. I'll have dinner ready. Don't forget the lucky pen."

"The what?"

"Your grandfather's pen? The only one you use for important contracts?"

"Oh…that. Yeah, of course. I won't forget."

Chapter Ten

Rawlston drove up to the front of Dahlia's house the next night, not sure if this was a good idea or not. But he *did* feel like he needed to make amends for his behavior by the cottonwood tree. He'd been petulant about the sheep getting under the fence, and then he'd blathered on about Dad and JoAnn. And moments later…they'd kissed. A kiss that rattled him right down to his core. Which suggested that it wasn't just the spiked punch that made his memories of their wedding night so steamy. They had some *wild* chemistry.

She called out when he rang the doorbell that the door was unlocked. Her house had a wide-open floor plan, with soaring cathedral ceilings. The great room included the large kitchen, a giant fieldstone fireplace, and a seating area divided into both dining and relaxing. There was also what seemed to be a reading nook, with a large, overstuffed chair and low bookcases below the windows. The deck and lakeshore were visible through the tall windows.

Dahlia was in the kitchen, her hair twisted into a messy knot on top of her head. She looked frazzled as she bent over in front of the open oven door, waving absently at an open bottle of wine and two glasses on the island.

"Help yourself. Sorry, I ended up running late and then I forgot about the roast while I was upstairs getting dressed." She straightened, wrinkling her nose. "I'm afraid it may be a little on the well done side by the time the veggies are cooked through."

He poured wine into the glasses, sliding one in her direction. "I'm sure it will be fine. What had you running late?"

"Peter Knight stopped by to look at Rebel. He said he was thinking of sending a few mares over for breeding in the spring."

Knight was another one of the top horse breeders in Texas. "Impressive."

She gave him a look, one eyebrow raised sharply. "Not terribly impressive, no."

"Why?"

She checked a pot on top of the stove. "He was a bit of an ass."

Rawlston suddenly saw red. "What the hell does that mean?"

She glanced back at him. "Relax, big guy. I just meant he was a misogynist. Very condescending about 'a pretty thing like me' handling a big, mean horse like Rebel, blah blah blah. He even tried to step up and take the lead from me when Rebel had one of his little tantrums, as if the guy had to save me. Which, of course, just fired Rebel up more." She huffed out a breath. "Knight was just generally annoying. Ah, I think the carrots and potatoes are done. Let's eat, and then you can sign those papers."

Despite his resolve to do the right thing, he did *not* want to sign off on the annulment yet. He told himself it was only because of Carter Powers, but he was beginning to think there might be another reason he wanted to stay married to Dahlia a while longer. He didn't want to examine that reasoning too deeply. Instead, he worked on keeping the conversation as far away from Vegas, annulment and signatures as possible. Surprisingly, it wasn't difficult. Just like that night at the reception, conversation flowed easily between them as they sat at the table to eat.

They talked about horses, sheep, cattle and what the plans were for the Fortunes' ranch. She asked about *his* ranch, and he told her what it was like to raise Brahman cattle and the fact that the house was nowhere near as grand as hers, but it was comfortable. He didn't mention how lonely it sometimes felt, especially since their return from Las Vegas.

Dahlia grew more animated as she spoke about her mother remodeling the Fortune castle into a boutique hotel and spa. Her siblings were all sliding into their roles on the ranch.

By the time she brought her homemade blueberry cobbler to the table for dessert, they'd moved on to more general topics—favorite books, movies, TV shows. It turned out that they were both slightly geeky. They ended up debating which space dramas were better, with him defending Star Wars as Dahlia argued for Star Trek.

He sat back in his chair and patted his stomach. "Woman, that was some damn fine cooking. That roast beef could be sold at the LC Club for top dollar."

She smiled, looking away as if to dismiss the compliment, but her cheeks went a pretty shade of pink. "Thanks. I loved spending time in the kitchen with Mom as a kid, and I picked up a few tricks. That was Angus beef, like what we'll be raising here on the ranch."

"Along with your sheep," he pointed out.

"Yes, along with them. Some people don't take the sheep very seriously, though."

"Your brothers?" That didn't sound like the Fortune guys. They were fiercely protective and supportive of each other and their sisters.

Dahlia started to answer, stopped, then finally spoke. "The boys have been good about it, and so have my sisters. Sabrina can't wait until we shear in the spring and she can get her hands on the wool for her knitting. It will be fun to create from product grown right here on the ranch."

He wondered who it was that wasn't taking her choice in livestock seriously. Which prompted him to ask if she was a knitter, too, but she shook her head. She pointed to a framed piece of art on the wall—a landscape with swirling shades of blue, green and brown, with mountains in the distance and a river flowing in the foreground.

"That's what I create with wool. And little things like those sleeping mice in the bowl on the buffet."

Rawlston was stunned. The mice were cute, and so realistic that, if he'd noticed them sooner, he might have thought they were real. But the landscape was incredible. He walked over for a closer look. Sure enough, it was wool, not paint, that created the scene on tightly stretched fabric.

"This is beautiful, Dahlia. Forget being a restaurant cook, you've found your calling as an artist. This should be in a museum somewhere." There was a smaller work in progress near the chair in the corner of the great room, and he went to check it out. It was a fall scene, more three-dimensional than the other work. A tall, dark tree was on one edge, with textured leaves on the branches and on the ground beneath it. He looked up to find her next to him. "Seriously—this stuff is good. No wonder you want to raise sheep. For you, they're raw material."

It was like looking at a whole new person. He'd had no idea she was an artist. He'd always thought of her as uptight, controlled, sharp. But no one like that could do anything like this—the sweeping, swirling colors, the texture, the *vision* to create something out of nothing. She was holding papers in her hand. *Oh, damn.* But she didn't hand them over. She was looking at him as if he'd just said something amazing. Surely she knew how good she was?

"Dahlia? I'm not exaggerating. This stuff is awesome."

"Not that many people have seen my pictures. I'm..." She blinked a few times. "I'm glad you like it."

She set the papers on the table and showed him how she worked the wool by stabbing at it with a long, barbed needle with a wooden handle. He'd never seen anything like it. He'd never seen anyone like *her.*

He helped her clean up the kitchen while she told him of picking up the hobby a few years ago when she was feeling stressed. Her dad was giving her a hard time about not coming to work for Windham Plastics and being a lowly groom instead, which he'd said was basically a "horse servant."

Rawlston had only met Casper Windham a handful of times, and on one of the occasions, the man had been scolding Dahlia for only placing third in a competition of thirty barrel racers. He was a hard man, and seemed especially so with his children. The polar opposite of Rawlston's own father. If anything, Keith Ames was *too* kindhearted. That was probably why he'd become so enamored with JoAnn—he believed the best of everyone.

Rawlston took Dahlia's soapy hands in his and looked her straight in the eyes. "You are no one's servant. I'm sorry he said that to you."

Her lips parted slightly, and it took all of his strength not to kiss her. But this wasn't the time for that. He needed his words to sink in, without distraction. She needed to know he thought her father was wrong about her. About a lot of things, but all Rawlston cared about was Dahlia.

It wasn't until he was driving home shortly after that he realized she'd never once asked him to sign those annulment papers.

"How could you *forget*?" Jade asked, accepting the coffee mug Sabrina handed her. The three sisters were in Sabrina's kitchen. It was two days since Rawlston had been to her house for dinner.

Dahlia waved her hand in a half-hearted shrug. "I don't know. We just got talking about stuff and I forgot to ask him to sign. And Lord knows, he isn't going to volunteer. I don't know why he's stalling, but he clearly is."

Sabrina sat down with Jade and Dahlia. "Has it ever occurred to you that he doesn't *want* to end the marriage? That maybe he likes being married to you?"

"He's *not* married to me!" Dahlia set her mug down with a thump. "I mean, yes, we're legally married, but we're not living as husband and wife. No one knows about it besides you two."

Jade snickered. "You mean you haven't snuck off for

one single kiss since spending your wedding night together in Vegas?"

Dahlia kept a straight face. At least she tried. She might have fooled Jade, but her twin could read her like a book. Sabrina leaned forward, staring straight at Dahlia.

"Oh my God, you *have* been sneaking kisses! What else have you two been doing?"

"Nothing!" Dahlia protested. "I swear, we haven't done anything. Other than argue."

Sabrina cleared her throat dramatically, and Dahlia conceded. "Okay, there was *one* kiss. Out on the range, by the big tree near the property line. It just…happened. We were talking and it was hot and—"

Jade snorted. "Oh, it was hot alright!" Sabrina joined in the laughter.

"We're not thirteen, ladies," Dahlia said. "You're overreacting to one simple kiss. He and I agreed it was a mistake that wouldn't happen again."

"And what about Carter?" Sabrina asked.

"What about him?"

Dahlia knew the reply was a mistake as soon as she said it. Her sisters' eyes went wide as they looked at each other and then to her, waiting for her to elaborate. She didn't want to tell them that she had been rethinking her relationship with Carter. Not because of Rawlston, or at least, not because she was falling for him or anything like that. But she couldn't get over the way he'd looked at her the other night when he saw her artwork, and how he'd been so horrified at one of her father's many criticisms of her.

Carter had never done either of those things. Not once. He'd dismissed her plans for raising sheep, mocked her artwork as a *cute little hobby*, and now he was rejecting the idea of even *living* in Chatelaine. She deserved a man who respected her choices the way Rawlston did, and she was beginning to realize Carter would never be that man.

"Dahlia?" Sabrina took her hand. "Are you and Carter over?"

"No!" She said it more forcefully than intended. "Nothing has changed."

"So you're still expecting a ring when he gets back from Europe?"

"Probably…"

She just wasn't sure she'd accept it. And not because of this wedding mess with Rawlston. She was having serious doubts about a future with Carter. But she couldn't discuss it with her sisters, because they were *not* impartial on the subject. They'd be thrilled if she admitted they'd been right about him all along. She needed to be sure before she dealt with their reactions.

"And… Rawlston?" Jade asked quietly.

"Rawlston is going to sign those papers. We got distracted and I forgot the other night, but that won't happen again. I'm going to his ranch this afternoon and I'll make sure I get his signature, with his *special lucky pen*, on the papers I've printed out for him. No more excuses."

She was surprised when she drove up to Rawlston's house. It was more humble than she'd expected—a smallish one-level stucco home in front of large cattle barns and a stable. He'd never been one to go for a flashy house or car. But she'd heard from her brothers that Rawlston had been successful when he took over his dad's ranch in Cactus Grove, and even more so with his Chatelaine ranch. She'd envisioned a different type of home—larger, newer, more upscale. Then again, Rawlston had been surprising her ever since he'd walked up to her in Las Vegas.

His dog came bounding off the front veranda as she got out of her car, barking loudly before rolling over on his back for a belly rub.

"Hi, Tripp!" She obliged with a scratch of his belly. "No sheep for you to chase today, huh?"

"I keep telling you that he's not a sheep dog, he's a cattle dog." Rawlston came around the corner of the house. "Come on inside, out of this heat."

It was another scorcher, with the temperature forecast to hit triple digits again. She grabbed her folder with the annulment documents from the car and followed him. From behind, she took in his broad shoulders. His long, confident stride. His light brown hair, curling from sweat and the heat. He was one of a kind. And she was married to him.

The house was at least fifty years old, but it was clean and neat inside. The large terracotta floor tiles and arched doorways gave it a Southwestern feel.

"This was built as the ranch foreman's house," Rawlston explained, giving her a quick tour. "This was all originally part of an even larger ranch, and their main house was on the lake. That burned down years ago and they never rebuilt. They sold the ranch instead."

She looked around and smiled. "This suits you."

His eyebrows rose. "Small and simple? Old and tired?"

"No. It's… practical. It has what you need, and nothing you don't."

"Fair enough. I figured I could always build a new

house on the ranch someday, but so far I haven't seen the need."

"Where does your foreman live?" Most ranches of this size had working cowboys on it.

"I'm pretty much the foreman," he answered with a shrug. "But I have a few local ranch hands who keep their horses here or trailer their own in."

"Again—practical," she pointed out. They were in the kitchen area, and there were plates set out with shredded lettuce, cooked ground beef, tomatoes, chilies, cheese and salsa.

"I put together a little taco bar for us for lunch. You want iced tea or beer?"

"Iced tea would be great, as long as it's not sweet tea."

"Something we have in common. I don't do sweet tea, either." He opened the refrigerator. "Grab a plate and help yourself."

They sat at the nearby table and laughed as they tackled their messy tacos. He'd added a shot of hot sauce to his, but she declined, letting him know she didn't think food should hurt you.

Just like the other night, they settled into easy conversation about the weather, his house, ranching and some casual Chatelaine gossip. She'd been getting to know some of her newfound Fortune cousins, and Rawlston knew most of them, too. He was actually good friends with West Fortune and his wife, Tabitha. They were raising one-year-old twins, which was apparently a Fortune family trait. Dahlia wondered aloud if it was her mother's Fortune genes that led to her giving birth to Sabrina and her.

"What's it like being a twin?" Rawlston asked. She'd been asked the question so many times.

"I don't know what it's like *not* to be a twin, so I never know how to answer that." She sipped her iced tea. "Sabrina and I definitely have a strong connection. I guess it's what they call *twin-sense*. But it's not magical— we're very in tune to each other's moods and stuff, but we don't read each other's minds. I got tossed and broke my arm when I was working at the race track, and she didn't suddenly feel the same pain or anything like that."

She looked up, surprised to see how intently he was listening. She always felt like she babbled uncontrollably around him, but he seemed genuinely interested. It was nice to not have to censor or edit herself around him. "Being a twin is complicated. On one hand, it's great to have someone who knows you so well and reads you like a book. But on the other hand, it can be stifling to have someone who's that close and who knows that much. It's hard to keep secrets."

He stared for a moment. "Does she know *our* secret?"

She felt a stab of guilt. "Um…yes. Sorry."

"Don't be." He lifted a shoulder and murmured matter-of-factly, "I figured you might have told her, being twins and all. I think it must be nice, having someone like that to share everything with."

"What's it like being an only child?"

"Just like being a twin, it's both a blessing and a curse." He refilled her tea, then set out a plate of warm sopaipillas for dessert. "You get lots of attention as a kid, and you hang out with adults a lot, so you grow up fast. But it can be lonely. And there's a level of pressure there. When you're the only child, you know you're all your parents have. You don't want to disappoint them, and when you *do* disappoint them, you can't point to a brother or sister and blame them. It's all you, all the time." He gave her a rueful grin. "I was jealous of all of you Windhams, with your big, noisy family full of kids."

It never occurred to her that anyone looked at her family as something to covet. She adored her siblings, but as a teen, it often felt that she had to compete for attention. It was easy to feel lost.

"And I was jealous of *you*, having a nice, quiet home with such calm, loving parents."

"I guess we always want what we don't have, right?"

Like the way she wanted *him* right now. Which was silly.

"Maybe so." She bit into a sopaipilla and moaned. "These are delicious!"

There was a heat simmering in his eyes as he watched her bite into the fried pastry that suggested he was thinking silly thoughts, too.

"Thanks." He cleared his throat sharply. "I picked them up this morning from a little Mexican cantina in town."

"Carlitas? Oh, I love that place. Their carnitas are next level." How interesting that they liked so many of the same things and places. "Another thing we have in common is that we both grew up with interesting names. Where did *Rawlston* come from?"

"It's my mother's maiden name. She was the last of her father's line of Rawlstons, and she wanted to carry the name on for at least one more generation. I don't mind it now, but it was a mouthful as a kid. It sounds so formal, and there isn't a good way to shorten it."

"Rolly?"

His eyes narrowed. "The kids who tried that one usually ended up with black eyes."

She laughed. "Message received. You know I feel the same about being called Dolly." Although it didn't sound so bad when Rawlston said it.

"Rolly and Dolly," he snorted. "We should put that on our wedding announcement."

"Oh, thanks for reminding me!" She turned to grab the folder from the countertop. "Get your lucky pen, mister. We're ending this marriage."

Chapter Eleven

Rawlston did his best not to make a sour face at his own stupid mistake in mentioning the marriage. He got up to search for a pen nice enough to be his "lucky" pen, and took his time doing it. The more time they spent together, the less he wanted to sign those papers, and he hadn't wanted to sign them in the first place.

The only thing that had changed was his reason for delaying. He still didn't want to think about Dahlia with Carter. But he was starting to *like* the idea of Dahlia with *him*. Despite his feelings about marriage, he was in no hurry to end this one.

While he "searched," she asked how he got Tripp, who was sprawled on the tile floor in the kitchen. The dog was usually there when the weather was this hot. The house had air-conditioning, but Rawlston didn't want to spend half his income keeping the temperature as low as his dog wanted. So Tripp took advantage of the cool tiles.

He told Dahlia how he'd gone to a friend's ranch outside San Antonio and had stumbled across a stall filled with a wiggling litter of puppies. Tripp had trotted over to Rawlston and sat down, looking up as if to say, *Here I am, Dad*. His friend Dan had tried to direct him to puppies with more energy, but Tripp just had a look that told Rawlston that he was the one. He'd been a great herding dog, and good companion, for three years now.

"Have you found that magic pen yet?" Dahlia asked sharply. He'd stopped pretending to look while talking about Tripp.

"It's not magic. It's just lucky." It also didn't exist. He fumbled around and finally pulled an old ballpoint pen from the junk drawer. "Here it is!"

He was running out of distractions to offer to keep her from getting his signature. She was standing now, her hand on the documents, staring at the pen in his hand.

"It's not exactly the fanciest lucky pen, is it?"

"Luck comes in all shapes and sizes."

The jig was finally up. He was going to have to sign the papers and annul their marriage. It was the right thing to do. He had no use for the institution, so delaying this any longer would be pointless anyway. He felt a small sense of relief at the idea that this performance would finally be over. The dishonesty was getting to him. He reached for the papers, and his pen clicked against the rim of his iced tea glass.

The glass flipped over in less than a heartbeat, sending iced tea all over the annulment papers. And he hadn't even been trying. Dahlia let out a cry, then tried to save the papers, but it happened too quickly. They were saturated with tea.

She glared at him as he tried to sop up the mess with a kitchen towel. "I swear you're doing this on purpose!"

He held his hand up to pledge his innocence. At least he wasn't going to have to lie about it. "Hand to God, that was an accident."

She stared hard, testing his sincerity and finally finding it acceptable.

"Fine. I can send a fresh copy to your printer. You got that fixed, right?"

"Uh...no." Technically, that wasn't a lie, either. He hadn't fixed it because it was never broken in the first place.

"Rawlston."

"Yes, Dahlia?"

"Every day makes me regret marrying you even more."

Dahlia was saddling Bunny to ride out to check the sheep when Bender shuffled into her stables. It was impossible to define the man's age. It could be anywhere between fifty and eighty, with his leathery skin and deep wrinkles that spoke of a lifetime on the range. He was short and stocky, and had an ambling walk, as if he'd spent so much time on horseback that his legs stayed in that position.

She and Bender were becoming pals. At first, it was because Bender was one of the few ranch hands who had experience with sheep. But she and he were developing a friendship built of mutual respect. He liked Rebel and the way Dahlia handled the stallion. In turn, she liked the way he could wade into a sea of sheep without spooking them. And could spot a potential problem in an instant.

Last week that problem had been parasites. Bender saw the telltale weight loss in a few ewes and lambs, and had singled them out of the herd for treatment. He'd held the sheep while instructing Dahlia how to administer the oral paste dewormer. That was one of the other things she liked about Bender——he treated her like an intelligent rancher, not a "pretty girl" who shouldn't be messing with livestock.

That was the phrase Carter had used in his email to Dahlia two days ago, after their tense exchange about living in Chatelaine. He clearly thought he was helping his cause by explaining that doing the gritty work of ranching wasn't going to be helpful to his campaign. It was fine if she wanted to be the "pretty girl on horse-back, or in front of a herd of cute sheep," but he didn't want her getting dirty, or ruining her "porcelain com-plexion" doing actual ranch work. The *last* thing Dahlia needed in her life was another opinionated man telling her what to want or how to behave.

Bender patted Bunny on the rump. "If yer ridin' the old mare for pleasure, go ahead. But don't worry about those sheep. I rode out and checked the herd this morn-ing, and they're all good. The medicine did the trick with the sick ones, and it doesn't seem to have spread."

"Oh...thanks, Bender," she replied. "You didn't have to do that, but I'm glad you did. And it's awful hot for a pleasure ride, so I'll let Bunny hang out here in the shade instead." She tugged the saddle off and put it on a nearby rack.

He shrugged. "I'm a ranch hand, and those sheep are on the ranch, so I reckon it's part of my job to check on 'em." He spit some chewing tobacco into the dirt. "I've been ridin' out there to count heads and see how they're doin' every morning since they got here. Mr. Arlo and Mr. Nash know and are okay with it. They told me that when it comes to the sheep, I report to you, not them."

Usually Dahlia was not keen on people taking care

of her business without her approval. But this didn't feel like that. This felt like her brothers knew she'd taken on a lot with basically an overnight herd of over a hundred sheep, and good old Bender had been keeping an eye on things. They were just looking out for her. Something she wasn't really used to.

Her brothers and sisters, of course, cared about her and would defend her against trouble in a heartbeat. But, sometimes, even siblings could be overbearing in their "caring." She thought of the time Jade had signed her up for theater class without telling her, because she thought Dahlia would be good at it. And of course there had been dear old Dad, who'd constantly pulled strings to get her better jobs with more prestige. He couldn't understand why she didn't want those *better* jobs with *better* people.

Maybe some of them would have been good opportunities for her, but she wanted to find those opportunities for *herself.* She didn't want them handed to her, or worse, her being bulldozed into them.

"Thanks so much, Bender. It's a relief to know I've got someone who knows what they're doing with sheep. It was ambitious of me to jump in with so many right off the bat."

Bender spit again. "The number don't make no difference really. Just more to count, but sheep are pretty independent. You're hiring shearers in the spring?"

"Yes, I'm already on their schedule. I wouldn't tackle that job myself."

"Smart. That's where people get themselves in trouble with sheep. They take too long, they stress the sheep, they get themselves hurt. The pros spend a couple minutes on a sheep, while amateurs waste half an hour or more. Multiply that by a hundred, and you're talking a week versus a day. Big difference."

Bender walked over to look at Rebel, who laid his ears back and made a false charge at the doorway. The ranch hand didn't flinch, so Rebel went back to eating his hay.

"Yeah, it's no fun to play those games with someone who's not afraid of you, is it?" Bender laughed at the stallion. "You're all bark, you big dummy."

"You've got his number. He's not exactly a marshmallow inside, but he's not the killer everyone tries to make him out to be."

"The best studs got some spirit in 'em. Don't need to be mean spirit, though. Just that big old ego that makes them act like cock of the walk." To her surprise, Rebel allowed Bender to scratch his neck, and then his head, although his eyes were still wide and cautious. "Oh, relax, big guy," Bender muttered. "You ain't impressin' me."

She put the mare back in her stall, then opened the gate to the covered outside run. The runs gave them more space to move around safely. She looked at the older man as she came back into the barn, latching the stall door behind her.

"Do you mind if I ask where you got the name Bender?"

He didn't look away from Rebel and the spot behind the horse's ear where he was lightly scratching with his fingertips in a rhythmic, circular motion. The stallion looked like he was in heaven.

"Cowboys love nicknames, Miss Dahlia. But you can't pick your own—it gets picked for ya'. I was a wild one in my younger days, and I liked my booze. Some mornings I came straight from the bar to the barn and saddled up without a wink of sleep." His voice was low and melodic, and she realized he was doing that for Rebel's sake, keeping the horse mesmerized. "One of the guys back then would say, *Bobby's been out on another bender*, and after he said it a few times, a nickname was born." He stepped back from Rebel's stall door and gave a shrug as he walked away. "Stuck on me for forty years now."

She did a quick calculation after he left. If he was old enough to drink, and had that nickname for forty years, Bender had to be around sixty, if not older.

Dahlia brushed dust off of her jeans and decided to visit her mother now that she had unexpected free time. Mom wasn't at the main house, so she drove to her mother's pet project—Fortune's Castle.

She pulled up in front of the place and stared at the unusual stone structure rising from the Texas dirt. It was an honest-to-God castle. Wendell Fortune had left it to his long-lost grandchild, Wendy Fortune. It had been a year of inheritances for Dahlia's mother. First, Casper Windham had died, and left most of his estate to Wendy. He'd sold Windham Plastics in the months before his death, so the amount was substantial for Mom and for all six of her children.

Then the Fortune castle and money had fallen into Mom's lap, along with a new name and new family. It had been…a lot. But Mom had handled all of the changes and surprises with her usual grace. That's who Wendy Windham Fortune was. She was always tasteful, kind, soft-spoken and almost ethereal in her mannerisms. But that gentle exterior hid a spine of titanium. She was strong-willed and smart. And knew what each person needed to hear in order to be persuaded to do her bidding, especially with her children.

"Hi, sweetheart!" Mom rushed out to give Dahlia a warm embrace. "I thought maybe you'd forgotten how to get here. I haven't seen you in a week." She held Dahlia at arm's length. "You look fabulous—the ranch life agrees with you. Do you have time for an early lunch? I can have the kitchen make up some sandwiches for us."

Dahlia was doing quick calculations in her head, cringing as she realized her mother was right—it had been over a week since she'd been here. The castle was only a short drive from the ranch—she drove past it every time she went into town. She'd been so distracted with the annulment and Rawlston's efforts to avoid moving forward with it that she'd lost track of the days.

"I'm sorry. It's been hectic. How are the renovations coming?"

"The renovations are making me pull my hair out," Mom answered. "But it's taking shape very nicely. You should stay for the afternoon. The Perry triplets were just here for a tour this morning—Haley's doing a story for the newspaper about our soft opening coming up. You know the three ladies, right?"

Dahlia had become friends with Haley, and had briefly met her sisters, Tabitha and Lily. She'd connected with Haley at a luncheon for new members of the Lake Chatelaine Business Owners Association, and they'd hit it off right away. The newspaper editor, Devin Street, had introduced them, and Haley had quietly filled her in on everyone's backstory-slash-gossip. She'd liked Haley's straightforward approach and dry humor. She was a very good observer of people. It was over a wine lunch last week that Haley had told her about a possible missing brother. The triplets didn't learn until recently about a rumor that claimed a *fourth* sibling might still be alive somewhere. According to an older woman who worked part-time at GreatStore, there'd been a baby Perry *boy* adopted out at birth. Were they quadruplets? Was he older? Younger? Did he exist at all?

The ladies were on the hunt for him, even though the old woman struggled with bouts of dementia. It could all be an elaborate fairy tale in her mind. Just in case, they'd done DNA testing to see if they could locate him through one of the popular genealogy companies.

"I can't stay long, Mom," Dahlia said, "but a quick lunch sounds nice."

They ate at a small table on a private stone veranda. The elaborate castle had hidden rooms and staircases, and was filled with quirky little clues built into the stones. The number fifty was a recurrent one—the number of men killed in a mining disaster back in the 1960s. It turned out that a woman had also died in the mine that day—Wendy's mother—leaving infant Wendy with a babysitter who'd raised her as her own. The true number of dead was fifty-one. Wendy had had the new number engraved into a stone on the veranda. They were sitting in the shade of a grape arbor, with a soft breeze to cool them. Dahlia sipped her tea, smiling to herself about her and Rawlston both being fans of the beverage in its pure form, without sugar.

"That's a secretive little smile you're wearing, Dahlia. Do you have a forbidden lover stashed away somewhere?"

She choked on her tea, laughing to hide her shock. "*Mom!* What on earth made you suggest that? I've been here for all of three weeks—hardly enough time to find a forbidden lover. Or a lover of *any* kind. I'm busy on the ranch, not running around dating a cowboy somewhere."

Unless she'd met him in Las Vegas and married him there, of course. But they weren't lovers. Not past that first night, except for one scorching kiss under a cottonwood tree.

Her mother was studying her now. "That was a long, detailed denial for a casual joke. What's going on with you?"

"Nothing." Dahlia did her best to look calm and composed. "There's nothing going on for me except lots of wooly sheep bouncing all over my range."

There was a long pause, Mom's examination unwavering.

"I don't believe you, Dahlia," she finally said, sitting up straight. "Spill it. Now."

If twin-sense was bad, mom-sense was even worse. She couldn't hide anything from her mother, and she no longer wanted to. She needed her mom's wisdom, and the only way she'd get it was to tell the truth.

"I sort of ran into Rawlston Ames in Las Vegas. We kind of got drunk and we…well—"

"Oh my God, you slept with him!" Mom exclaimed, looking surprisingly happy at the thought.

"Well…" Dahlia let out a long sigh, then told the story as quickly as possible. "Only *after* we got married. In a hot pink chapel in a midnight ceremony neither of us remembers very well."

Wendy Fortune froze, her tea glass just an inch from her mouth, which was now wide-open in shock. She slowly set down her glass, and all the while her forehead was wrinkled in deep thought as she stared at Dahlia.

"You…and Rawlston…*married*?"

Dahlia nodded. "Believe me, no one was as surprised as him and me the next morning. And no one knows about this, except Sabrina and Jade. We're getting it annulled, of course."

"Why?"

Now it was Dahlia's turn to look shocked. "*Why?* Well, for one thing, I barely know the man. I've hardly seen him since high school. For another, we were drunk out of our minds on spiked punch. And most importantly, I'm dating *Carter*, Mom!"

A brief flash of some emotion crossed her mother's face. There'd been the tiniest wrinkle of her nose in distaste, and the lines around her mouth had deepened as if she was struggling to maintain her composure. Did *everyone* dislike Carter? Was it possible that Dahlia had been so wrong about him? Or had been in such denial, which seemed more feasible? Her mother reached out to take her hands.

"Tell me how this all happened."

She did, skipping over the hot wedding night of lovemaking, and the kiss out on the range. She told how fate seemed to be conspiring against Rawlston signing the papers, with one thing after another going wrong.

"Are you sure it's fate interfering, and not Rawlston?"

She'd wondered the same thing, but it made no sense. "Rawlston despises the institution of marriage, Mom. His first marriage was a hot mess, and there's no way he wants to stay hitched to me. I think we've just had bad luck."

"And what about you and Carter?"

"Well…" It was a very good question. "He's been dropping a lot of hints lately, and I'm expecting him to propose when he gets home."

"That's a very factual description of your status together. Do you love him?"

"I…uh…" Dahlia's shoulders slumped. "I'm honestly not sure, but I think we make a good couple—on paper, at least." They were both wealthy, successful, mature adults who had ambitions for their lives. Those ambitions were completely different, though. That was becoming more and more apparent every time they communicated.

Her mother patted her hands before releasing them and sitting back. "The problem is, people don't *live* on paper, dear. And your voice has no excitement at all when you speak about Carter. But when you talk about Rawlston, you sound—"

"Irritated? Frustrated?"

"Maybe." Mom paused. "But at least those are *real* emotions. The kind of emotions that keep you awake at night, thinking about the man. Does Carter make you feel that way?"

She didn't hesitate.

"No, he doesn't."

"But the man you're married to does?"

"Mom, we can't build a relationship on irritating each other!"

Her mother smiled that all-knowing mom-smile of hers. "You'd be surprised what you can build a relationship on, Dahlia."

Chapter Twelve

Rawlston gave two short whistles, sending Tripp scurrying around the left flank of the cattle. The dog nipped at a few heels, deftly dodging some corresponding kicks, and started the herd moving away from the fence line. It had become an almost daily routine with this subset of his overall herd. They loved coming to the top of the hill between the Fortune and Ames ranches and grazing with however many of Dahlia's sheep managed to scurry under the barbed wire and onto his property. It was as if the cows and sheep had become friends somehow, and he couldn't afford to let that happen. Every rancher knew that cattle and sheep didn't mix.

He nudged Malloy forward, and between the horse and Tripp, the cattle moved into a jog away from the hilltop and back down to the level ground, where there was also plenty of grazing. Rawlston's fear was that the sheep would eventually wander this far, and end up ruining some of the best grazing ground he had. He turned to ride back to the house.

It had been three days since he'd innocently spilled iced tea on the annulment papers. He was surprised Dahlia hadn't been back the next morning with a fresh

set, but so far she'd stayed away. Salty old Bender Grant
had been checking the sheep for her. Rawlston had seen
him yesterday and this morning, riding through the herd,
counting heads. He was glad to see she was getting some
help. Dahlia had always been so fiercely independent,
scorning other people's help and advice. Not that that had
ever stopped her brothers and sisters from offering it.

Just yesterday, he'd run into her sister, Jade, at Great-
Store. He'd nodded when they'd made eye contact, figur-
ing she'd go on her way without stopping. They barely
knew each other. But she'd rushed over to him, wide-
eyed and animated.

"Rawlston! Oh, it's so good to see you! How's everything on your ranch these days?"

"Uh…fine. And how are you doing, Jade? Settling in
okay in Chatelaine?"

"Yes. It's been a big change, but I like it here." She'd
looked around the giant box store and wrinkled her nose
the same way her sister liked to do. "I wish the shopping
was better, but other than that, it's all good."

He'd nodded. "We have everything we need, but not
much more than that."

She'd given him a funny look, which made him un-
easy, then put her hand on his arm. Another trait like
Dahlia's.

"Okay, I won't beat around the bush here." She'd
glanced around to make sure no one else was in the
canned food aisle. "I know what happened in Vegas."

He wasn't thrilled that Dahlia had told another of her
siblings about the wedding she wanted kept secret. He
rushed to reassure Jade.

"We're getting it annulled."

"Don't."

"What?"

Jade had given him a conspiratorial wink. "You seem to be dragging your feet on the annulment, and I think you should keep stalling for, say…" she'd looked up in thought "…maybe another month?"

"Until after Carter gets home." Her eyes had brightened when he hit on the truth.

"Something like that, yes." She'd looked around again. "Is that why you've been avoiding signing anything?"

"It was, originally, yes. But it doesn't feel right. She and I screwed up, and I can't use that mistake to interfere with what she wants."

"Sure you can." Jade's laughter had brightened. "Her and Carter are all wrong for each other, and you know it. He's another Casper Windham, and that's the last thing Dahlia needs in her life. Her relationship with our father was messy, and she let him get into her head. If you don't sign the papers, she can't say yes to Carter when he gets back."

He'd told Jade the delay felt like a wasted effort, since Dahlia would just run to Carter as soon as the annulment went through. The thought ate at him like acid, but she had the right to make her own choices, and his tactics had been making him squeamish lately.

"Carter's not the waiting around kind," Jade had pointed out. "He has a very short attention span. He'll move on before she can finish asking him to wait."

She'd probably been right about Carter, but Rawlston hadn't made her any promises about the annulment. The more he got to know Dahlia, the more he liked and respected her. Then again, if she was the type to prefer Powers, then maybe he didn't know her all that well after all.

His father's truck was at the ranch when he got back. Dad got out of the driver's side, and someone opened the passenger door. Dad had brought JoAnn here, to Rawlston's home. He remembered what Dahlia had said to him—he couldn't hold it against JoAnn that she wasn't like his mother. He'd done some digging, and she seemed to be exactly who she'd said she was. JoAnn Henderson from Rockslide, Vermont. A widow who'd been running a farm stand for years—first with her husband, then alone after he'd died.

Tall and buxom, she looked up at Rawlston with a hesitant smile as he rode Malloy over to the car. Dad walked to her side, giving him a warning look as if to say, *Be careful, son.* Rawlston dismounted and greeted them.

"Dad, JoAnn. Did we have something planned today?"

"Nah," Dad said. "I was telling JoAnn about the ranch and decided I should show it to her—" he gave a pointed look "—rather than wait for an invitation."

"Oh, yeah. Sorry. It's been busy and..." He floundered for an excuse and finally gave up. "Come on in. I'll throw some burgers on the grill for us." He turned to JoAnn, who was carefully keeping her distance. She was giving him his space, respecting his doubts about her. Which made him feel like a jerk. His dad was determined to marry this woman, and Rawlston needed to at least *try* to honor that. He smiled at her. "Come on in, JoAnn. Just uh…forgive the mess, okay? The house is nothing fancy."

She seemed to relax a bit. "Rawlston, I lived in a hundred-and-eighty-year-old Vermont farmhouse most of my adult life. I don't give a hoot about fancy *anything*."

They ended up having a nice afternoon. His dad told stories about raising Rawlston in Cactus Grove, and JoAnn talked about her two children. Her son was in Maine, and her daughter lived in a Boston suburb. She had three grandchildren, and Rawlston didn't miss the look his father gave him. He wouldn't mind giving his dad a grandchild or two, but it wouldn't be happening anytime soon. JoAnn insisted on clearing the table after they ate, and while she was out of earshot he got another one of those looks from Dad.

"What?" he asked. "You're obviously dying to say something, so just…say it."

"I'm wondering how your, uh, marriage is going."

"It'll be going away pretty soon. We have the annulment papers, and just have to get them signed and sent back to the lawyers."

"You sure you want to do that?"

He wasn't, but he didn't want to admit that to his father. Or to himself. "It needs to be done, Dad. She wants someone else. Story of my life."

"Quit feeling sorry for yourself, son. Not every woman is Lana."

"What's the point of marriage, anyway?" Rawlston complained. "Mom was your one and only, and now that she's gone, along comes JoAnn, who's the complete opposite of everything you loved in Mom, and you're going to marry *her*. It makes no sense to me."

His father's face was stony and silent for a long moment. Then he slowly shook his head. "Boy, you really don't get it, do you? JoAnn has the same exact quality

I loved in your mother—she's genuine. She is who she is, through and through. Her version of being genuine is admittedly different from Kathy's, but their honesty and openness are identical. There weren't any games with your mother, and there aren't any with JoAnn, either." He leaned forward to make his point, staring straight at Rawlston. "I initially thought I wanted to be with JoAnn because we were compatible and I was lonely. But now that she's here, in person... Well, I didn't think it could happen again, but... I'm falling in love with her."

Rawlston was surprised, but his dad had always been a romantic. "Aren't you afraid you might be setting your-self up for heartbreak? I mean... Mom was sick. You told me JoAnn's a breast cancer survivor, and..." He felt like a jerk for even bringing it up.

"And she could get sick again?" Dad nodded slowly. "She could. Or I could. Or *you* could. None of us knows what the future holds. There's no guarantee of happily-ever-afters for any of us. Falling in love is probably the biggest gamble a person can take. But the rewards are so great that it's worth it."

"It wasn't for me."

"The problem with you and Lana was that you were in love with different things. You were in love with *her* and she was in love with *marriage*. She was a borderline bridezilla about your wedding, spending a fortune so she could be a fairy-tale princess. She envisioned the fairy tale *after* the wedding, too—picket fence, two kids and a dog, hubby coming home every night. And as it turned out, she wasn't built for sitting around alone while you went off and had your adventures at sea."

He wasn't wrong. Lana had thrown huge red flags

during the wedding planning. She'd told him more than once that it was *her* day, and refused to listen to his opinion that it should be *their* day. But his friends had assured him all women wanted to be the star of their wedding.

He thought of Dahlia in that ridiculous electronic veil in a bright pink chapel in Las Vegas. Completely at ease and in the moment. Yes, they'd been drunk, but he had a feeling that was who Dahlia was. What was the word Dad used? *Genuine.*

"Son," his father started, "you need to find someone to love who loves you back. *Then* you'll understand why people want to be married."

"Yeah, well...that's not Dahlia." If he thought there was a chance with her, what would he do?

"Maybe not. But don't close the door on her until you know that for sure."

He was going to argue that *she* was the one closing the door, but JoAnn rejoined them and he let the subject drop. After they'd left, he sat on the patio and sipped a good Southern whiskey, wondering what a *real* marriage to Dahlia would be like.

Dahlia hadn't been to the Daily Grind since that first meeting with Rawlston. Going out for breakfast wasn't her thing. But Haley had invited her to breakfast, and she'd decided forging a new friendship was worth a change in her routine. Haley said Dahlia needed to be seen in the Daily Grind if she wanted to be considered a local.

"The LC Club is great for networking with the upper crust, but the heart of the real Chatelaine beats inside places like the Longhorn Feedstore and the Daily

Grind," Haley said. "Sit with Beau Weatherly and ask him a question or two. Make friends with Sylvie. You're a rodeo gal, so they'll accept you in no time at all. And once you're accepted, *all* the doors will open for you."

Dahlia had loving brothers and sisters, but she'd left her few close friends behind in Cactus Grove, and she was missing them. A woman needed a friend who wasn't family. Otherwise, who on earth would she talk to *about* her family? And sometimes, a person needed to do that, no matter how much she loved her siblings.

So here she was, walking into the Daily Grind at 7 a.m., ready for coffee. She'd opted for ranch wear—jeans, her everyday boots and a blue gingham Western shirt. This was who she was, and she didn't want to network as anyone other than herself. Beau Weatherly was seated in the corner, with his Free Life Advice sign on the table. A woman was sitting with him and they were laughing over something. A man waited patiently for his turn with Beau.

Rawlston had told her Beau's unusual story. He'd been a successful rancher and an even more successful investor. He had a sixth sense about which businesses were going to take off and which ones had run their course. He and his wife had built themselves a wonderful life on a spacious ranch in Chatelaine. Then Susan Weatherly had died unexpectedly, leaving Beau wallowing in grief. His wife had been a big believer in giving back to the community. It was her way of paying it forward and sharing their bounty with others.

Beau started coming to the Daily Grind to be around other people, and customers would ask him for his advice on things. He enjoyed sharing his wisdom, and pretty soon people were coming to the coffee shop just to see Beau. With the shop's permission, he made his appearances official, coming in most mornings to answer whatever questions people had. Rawlston had explained that sometimes his advice was tongue-in-cheek, like when people asked if it was going to rain that day, and he'd answer, *It's gonna rain somewhere, for sure.*

It was a sweet gesture that had become a beloved tradition. And it had apparently helped Beau as much as it had helped the town. It gave him a reason to get up in the mornings, and Rawlston said Beau had seemed more like his former happy self in recent months.

Dahlia had just taken a seat when her phone pinged with a text. It was Haley, telling her she couldn't make it because the paper was covering a story about an overnight house fire somewhere. She told Dahlia to "mingle," but that felt too much like political schmoozing. She wasn't running for office—she just wanted to get to know people here. She ordered a large cappuccino and a raspberry scone, which arrived drenched in butter and smelling heavenly. She'd just taken her first bite when she made eye contact with Beau, two tables away.

He gave her a smile and a nod before turning back to the young man at his table. There was no one left in line. She thought about getting up to wait, but that felt silly. Dahlia didn't need anyone's advice, and she didn't want anyone thinking she did.

Taking another bite of the delicious scone, she looked over toward Beau's table and found him watching her again. The young man was gone. No one was waiting. Beau smiled and nodded at the empty chair, inviting her to join him. Knowing it would be rude to refuse, she gathered her plate and mug and moved to his table.

He jumped to his feet to hold the chair. "Good morning, Dahlia. I know who you are, but it's nice to meet you in person. I'm—"

"Beau Weatherly," she finished for him. "Everyone knows who you are, Mr. Weatherly."

"Everyone also knows to call me Beau. What brings you to the coffee shop at this early hour?"

"I was supposed to meet Haley Perry, but she had to cancel."

He shook his head. "That gal is always on the run. She's a good'n, though. How are those sheep of yours doing?"

"They're doing well, thanks." She wasn't sure how much to share with him.

"And the ranch is doing well for your family?"

"Oh, yes. We're still settling in, but it's good."

He stared at her for a long moment.

"Then what's troubling you?"

She straightened. "Nothing! Everything's fine." Then she realized why he was asking. "Oh, I didn't come over for advice, Beau. No offense—I'm sure you're great at it, but I'm okay."

He stared again, then smiled as he set his coffee mug down. "If you say so, Dahlia. But let me give you some free advice anyway." He waved Sylvie over for a refill, then waited for her to leave, which the older woman did reluctantly.

Dahlia had no idea what kind of advice a total stranger thought she needed. But his eyes were warm and kind. Almost…fatherly. The idea shocked her. She didn't even realize she'd been *looking* for a father figure. But here she was, staring at Beau Weatherly, wishing she'd had a dad like him. And feeling guilty about it.

"Thanks, but I... I should go." Emotions welled up in her, and she needed time to sort through them.

"I understand." Beau's smile deepened. "Let me just say this—it's good to keep an open mind when life puts a chance at happiness in front of you. It might not be the future you imagined or even one you think you want, but life is funny that way." He winked. "Have a good day, Dahlia, and remember—love shows up in the strangest places."

Chapter Thirteen

Rawlston was going to sign those papers. He drove onto the Fortune ranch and headed for Dahlia's house at the end of the road. She wasn't expecting him, but he couldn't keep dragging this out, despite what his father had said about fate and all that nonsense. If anything, it was because of those comments. If Dad wanted to marry JoAnn, fine. Fine for *Dad*. But the conversation had reminded Rawlston that marriage wasn't for him, and he couldn't keep up this charade any longer.

Dahlia had stopped pressuring him about the annulment lately, but he had a feeling that was just reverse psychology. Pestering him constantly hadn't worked, so now she was backing off, making him come to her. And it was working, because here he was, driving to her house unannounced. He imagined the surprise on her face when she opened the door at this late hour to find him standing there, pen in hand. Tonight she was going to get exactly what she wanted.

He saw lights on in the stable, and slowed. Her golf cart was outside the barn door. It was after nine o'clock, and he grew concerned. Was something wrong with one of the horses? Or was it the sheep? He parked his truck by the barn and walked to the open door. Dahlia was there, with the paint stallion standing on the crossties. She was brushing Rebel slowly down his neck and shoulders, almost like a massage, and she was speaking low and soft. The stallion, normally fidgety and raring to go, looked surprisingly mellow, with one hind leg relaxed and his head down, eyes half-closed.

Rawlston took another step forward, then heard Dahlia say his name. To the horse. He paused to listen.

"I just don't get it, Rebel. What is it about Rawlston that makes my pulse jump like a jackrabbit every time we touch? I know we were drunk in Vegas, but if it had been anyone else in the world, I can't imagine going so far as to *marry* them. Rawlston just felt...*safe*, you know what I mean?" The brush moved rhythmically over the big horse's coat. "And I don't mean safe in a boring way. He's got this laid-back-dude thing going, but at the same time, he pushes me. Or pushes my buttons, at least. None of it makes any sense, but I just can't help wanting to be with him. Wanting to be in his arms. It's stupid, right?"

Rawlston stepped into the light from the doorway. "I don't think it's stupid."

She spun, and the quick movement had Rebel laying his ears back in agitation. Rawlston had interrupted a perfectly good massage, and the horse was clearly not happy about it. But Rawlston's eyes were on Dahlia, and only her. There was a blush of pink on her cheeks, and her perfect lips were parted just enough for him to know she was feeling the same aching desire that he was. Then her eyes narrowed.

"You scared ten years off my life! What are you doing here?"

He closed the distance between them. "I couldn't stay away."

"Are you *drunk*?"

"Not this time, Dahlia…" He slid one hand behind her head and the other behind her back. He waited, needing to be sure before he made another move. She stared up at him, then moved closer, stepping into his embrace. "You wanted to be in my arms, and now you are. What's next?"

Her eyes deepened to blue velvet, and her arms slid around his neck.

"Now we kiss," she whispered.

And they did. Gently at first, with their lips caressing and their tongues tangling in a slow, sultry dance. Neither one of them was in a hurry, and it made the kiss all the more satisfying. She let out a soft moan as she turned her head to give him easier access. He took advantage of it, taking her mouth and tasting the heat of her desire. She wanted this. She wanted *him*. And he was very much okay with that.

His arms tightened around her, lifting her from the floor as the kiss turned more frantic. She hooked one long leg around his hips and he tugged her higher until both of her legs were wrapped around him. He gripped her tightly and she moaned again, grinding against his hardness.

Spots of bright colors burst behind his tightly closed eyes. For the first time since he was a teen, he worried about losing control before he ever got his clothes off. She was setting him off like a firecracker.

"The house," he muttered, nibbling on her neck as he gasped for air.

"The horse," she answered breathlessly. "Let me put Rebel away. Put me down. And then—" she clasped his face between her hands "—*then* we go to the house."

She ushered the stallion back into his stall, and Rebel rolled an annoyed look at Rawlston as he passed him. Rawlston accepted responsibility for the horse's interrupted grooming session, and had no remorse. Zero. None. Dahlia had barely latched the stall door when Rawlston turned her and pressed her back against it, kissing her hard. She returned the kiss just as eagerly, then whispered against his ear.

"Too many clothes..."

When the lady was right, she was right. They *did* have too many clothes on. He tossed off his T-shirt and helped her tug her blue knit top over her head, revealing a lacy pink bra that matched the soft blush high on her cheeks. They both froze, staring at each other hungrily. She was the first to reach out, tracing her fingers in a zigzag pattern down his chest, flicking at his nipples with her fingernails, sending a jolt of electricity down his spine. His shorts were suddenly uncomfortably tight, and he growled a curse as he grabbed her wrist and pulled her close.

It was his turn to tease *her* breasts now, and she let out a cry as her head fell back. She bit her lower lip as he ran his tongue around and around before settling his lips on the peak and drawing her into his mouth, right through the lace. She hooked her leg around his thigh again, getting herself closer to where he was pulsing inside his shorts, desperate to be inside of her.

But not here. Barns were only good for sex in the movies. The reality? Hay was scratchy, not soft. And full of bugs and spiders. Besides, it was hot out here, and not the sexy kind of hot. The sun may have gone down, but the air was thick and still with humidity. There was a tropical storm spinning somewhere out in the Gulf of Mexico, and it was pushing hot, charged air into Texas. He'd heard thunder rumbling in the distance when he'd walked to the barn. Besides, making love while her horses looked on was a bit of a buzzkill.

"House!" He gasped the word against her skin before taking one more lap around her right breast.

"Yes!" she cried. He wasn't sure if it was agreement or ecstasy. She pushed on his shoulders. "Let's *go*."

It was a wild dash to the house. But unlike Las Vegas, he remembered every single detail. Their lips were locked together most of the trip, as clothes went flying. Their shirts were in the barn. Her bra landed somewhere outside. They jumped on the golf cart, where she strad- dled his lap as he tried to drive. She tugged his belt off and tossed it somewhere in the dark, then buried her fin- gers in his hair and kissed him so hard he almost drove into a pomegranate tree in her yard.

He wasn't exactly sure when her boots came off, but when they stopped in front of the lakeside house, she'd stepped out of her jeans easily, kicking them into the shrubbery in her bare feet. *His* boots came off in her doorway, with one landing outside on the porch and the other inside the door. Her panties and his boxer briefs left a trail down the hallway to her bedroom.

He barely registered the room she led him into. It was big. There were windows. The only thing he cared about was the king-size bed. He tossed her onto it and climbed on, kneeling over her like a starving man staring at a feast. Before he could get any closer, she held her hand up, her fingers against his mouth. He went still. *Oh, damn.* Too much? Too fast?

"Condoms." She tipped her head in the direction of an arched doorway. "Bathroom. Bottom drawer."

He closed his eyes in relief. She wasn't stopping what was happening. She was just being smart about it. He could live with that. Because he really, truly, absolutely did not want to stop.

Dahlia watched Rawlston's very fine ass vanish into the bathroom, then heard him opening and closing doors and drawers frantically.

"Bottom drawer!" she called out, but before she finished, he was hurrying back to the bed, a length of condom packets hanging from his hand. She couldn't help chuckling. "Feeling optimistic, are we?"

He tore one off and tossed the rest onto the nightstand. "I've always been a positive thinker, babe."

He rolled the condom on, then settled his weight over her. She'd pushed back against the pillows, and he held himself up on extended arms, his hips against hers, his erection twitching between her legs. She closed her eyes in anticipation, but then…nothing happened. She opened them to find him staring at her.

"What's wrong?" she asked.

"Nothing at all is wrong. This is…" He looked down at her naked beneath him. "This is everything I've dreamt about for weeks now. It's perfect. But…what are we doing? Are you sure we're okay here…"

There was a flash of light, and thunder boomed outside the windows. Even the weather was turned on.

She reached up to cup his cheek with her hand. "I know consent may have been a little sketchy on our wedding night, for both of us. But I'm stone-cold sober tonight, and I think you are, too." He nodded as she continued. "I'm fully capable of making decisions for myself. I want this, Rawlston. I want *you*."

"Thank Christ." He entered her as his mouth covered hers, capturing her cry.

All those fragmented memories of that night in the Las Vegas suite came together in her mind like a Rubik's Cube snapping together in perfect symmetry. He moved inside of her, nipping the skin at the base of her neck as they rocked together, building a fire that became the center of her universe. She reveled in the realness of this moment with him. Vegas had seemed like a dream—something that couldn't possibly have been that good. But here she was, with Rawlston, feeling that fire building and feeling a scream rising up inside of her. Like she was trying to contain an explosion that wouldn't be stopped. This couldn't be happening. It couldn't be *Rawlston* who made her feel this way.

She clung to him as they both fell off a cliff of urgent, magnificent passion that consumed them both. Why weren't the sheets on fire? Why weren't the smoke alarms going off? Why wasn't there a choir of angels singing in her bedroom?

Dahlia was barely coherent when a flash of lightning lit up the room again, followed quickly by a crackle of thunder that seemed to rumble on indefinitely. Was it real, or had their lovemaking made her dream up the sudden storm? Rawlston shuddered in her arms, then collapsed against her with a loud groan.

"Damn, woman. I guess it wasn't just the spiked punch that made us so good together. We're the real deal."

She wanted to argue, but couldn't. She'd never had a man's touch light her up the way Rawlston's did. There was something deep between them. Something unlike anything she'd ever felt before. It was thrilling. And terrifying. She shivered, and he reacted immediately.

"You okay?" He slid off her and pulled her into his arms, his warmth chasing away any doubts for now.

"I think so. It's just…that was…a lot."

"Too much a lot, or the kind of a lot that makes you want more?"

"The second. But I'm not sure if I *should* want more. Rawlston…"

He snuggled her in close, resting his head on hers. "It's okay, babe. We'll figure this out together." She closed her eyes and absorbed his warmth. He was her safe place. He was…home.

Chapter Fourteen

Rawlston woke up alone, in a strange room. He blinked a few times in the darkness before he realized he was in Dahlia's bed. Just like in Vegas, their lovemaking had scrambled his brain. And something else that was just like Vegas—they'd been *incredible* together.

He lay back against the pillow, remembering every detail this time around. Every touch. Every look. Every whisper and every cry. They knew what to do to please each other without saying a word, and they both focused on that—pleasing the other person. Was he physically satiated and happy? Of course. But he felt far more satisfaction knowing that he'd absolutely rocked her world tonight.

At least…that's what he'd thought. But she wasn't in the bed. And the bathroom was dark. He got up and looked for his shorts, then remembered they'd shed their clothes last night like Hansel and Gretel had left a trail of crumbs. He snagged a towel and wrapped it around his waist, following the soft light out on the deck, which he could see through the bedroom's open French doors.

Dahlia was curled up on one of the upholstered lounge chairs near the gas-fueled firepit, where low blue flames rose up through clear glass pebbles. Wearing a very short pink robe, she was sitting in the covered section of the deck, away from the rain that was falling now. Thunder rumbled in the distance—another round of storms were rolling in.

"Hey," he said, not wanting to startle her.

She lifted her head and stared at him for a moment before nodding back. "Hey."

He thought she might be looking for alone time, but she slid over in the lounge, making room for him to join her. He did, wrapping his arms around her and pulling her close, her back to his chest. "You okay?"

"I'm not sure." She'd almost whispered the words. "I mean, yes—there's nothing wrong with me. Like I said before, it's—"

"A lot?" He finished the sentence for her. "Yeah, I know. We're pretty amazing together, Dahlia."

She snorted. "Yes, we are." She pulled away so she could look him in the eye. "But what does that mean?"

He shrugged. "Does it have to mean anything other than that? Just because we can't define it, that doesn't mean it's a bad thing."

She relaxed back against him again, staring at the flames. "No, but it's not necessarily *good*, either. It's... unexpected. I'm not big on surprises, and what we have going on is a huge surprise to me."

He kissed the top of her head. "Me, too."

It was one thing to nurse a crush from high school. But he'd never in his horniest dreams thought they'd be *this* good together. That she'd be the one woman to shatter him in bed and put all the pieces back together so he was better than before. What she'd done to him was magic, pure and simple. And he wanted it to happen again. Right now. And again after that, because he had a feeling he'd never, ever have enough of her.

"So what happens now?" she murmured.

"If you're asking what I *want* to have happen now, then my answer is we go back to bed and do that all over again. More than once. Slower. Faster. Harder. Softer. I don't care—I just know I need more of whatever that was." She didn't answer right away, and he started to worry. "Only if you're interested, of course."

She turned onto her back, sliding her arms up around his neck as he leaned over her. "I'm interested. I'm *terrified*, but I'm interested. My only question is—" Her back arched up toward him. "Why do we need the bed?" Lightning flickered across the sky, and Rawlston groaned, suddenly hard and aching for her. *Yes, please. Right here!*

He kissed her, softly at first, then growing in intensity. She pressed her body against his, and he wasn't sure if it was thunder he heard or if it was his pulse pounding in his ears. He worked her robe open and she shrugged out of it as he tossed his towel aside. They fit together so perfectly. The new storm grew closer, and he couldn't imagine anything better than this—making love to Dahlia outdoors with a Texas storm brewing. Except for one thing…

"Damn it," he moaned through gritted teeth. "Condom."

There was a beat of silence before she answered. "I'm on the pill, Rawlston."

He lifted his head. "Are you saying what I think you're saying? You want to…?"

"I'm healthy and I assume you are, too. I have birth

control taken care of. Technically, we are husband and wife, so…"

"Oh, hell yes."

He was on top of her, and then inside of her, in seconds. His eyes closed at the feeling of skin against skin, warm and wet. It was all enough to make him lightheaded for a second, but a mist of rain brushed across his back and snapped him back to reality. The wind was gusting, sending soft sheets of warm rain under the roof of the deck and onto the lounge. There was another flash of lightning, much closer and brighter.

Dahlia looked up at him, her eyes wide and dark, shining with intensity. She might be as turned on by the storm as she was by him. He began to move in her, and she raised her legs and wrapped them around his waist. The position made it even easier to thrust inside her, and he did. She called out his name as she met him move for move. Soon he wasn't sure what was real and what wasn't. Was it raining? Was that thunder? Was the wind moving things on the deck, or was that all part of the vortex that was him and Dahlia?

He held back as long as he could, waiting for the storm to be right over them. Waiting for her to beg him for release. Both things happened at once, and not a moment too soon. With a garbled yell, he came in her, quivering and thrusting again and again, until there was nothing left to him. Nothing but Dahlia, still wrapped around him, making soft purring sounds of joy.

"Christ, woman." He tried to gather his wits, but they were scattered in the wind.

"I know," she answered, gently patting his back, now

damp from the rain and wind. "That was even better than earlier. Better than Vegas. The hands-down best."

"Best between us or your best ever?" He couldn't help asking. She gave him a throaty laugh, then kissed his neck.

"Both."

Rawlston smiled in quiet pride. "Best sex ever, eh?"

"Yes, you egomaniac," she laughed. "A new benchmark has been achieved. Wanna see if we can break it before the sun rises?"

"I've heard trying is where the fun is, so why not?"

They made love again on the lounge chair, then went back to her bedroom for more fun before collapsing in each other's arms in complete exhaustion. She was sprawled across him in a position nearly identical to that morning in Las Vegas. He ran his fingers through her hair and down her back, and her skin twitched like a cat. She moaned something that ended with his name, but he didn't pick up on the first few words. He only knew she sounded happy.

Rawlston shifted so that he could hold her in an embrace, and she reciprocated without waking, sliding her arms around his body as she snuggled close. This was a brand-new sensation for him—a mix of physical pleasure and emotional contentment so intense that it scared him. Partly because he was afraid it wouldn't last. And partly because he was afraid it would, which would mean changing all of his most firmly held beliefs on women, relationships and marriage.

He'd been convinced he didn't need or believe in any of it. Until tonight, when Dahlia showed him what a future with her might look like. And he, like an addict, was ready to fight to keep it.

To keep *her*.

Dahlia woke to the sun streaming through her bedroom windows. She blinked a few times, wondering why the sun was so bright. Then she checked the time and sat up abruptly. Eight o'clock? That wasn't possible. She *never* slept this late. She scrambled out of bed and into the bathroom to splash water on her face and untangle her hair, which looked like she'd been making crazy love all night long. She paused, staring at her reflection, expecting to see more of a change than messy hair. Nope. Same Dahlia looking back at her. But on the inside, she was a different woman.

All because of Rawlston Ames.

Her bed was empty, but she knew he was still here. She could hear him whistling in the kitchen, and heard pans and dishes being moved around out there. Smiling to herself, she pulled a cotton sundress over her head then went looking for him. His back was to her as he worked at the stove. He wasn't wearing a shirt, and his shorts were unbuttoned and hanging low on his hips.

"I could get used to this." In more ways than one— the breakfast *and* the view.

He glanced over his shoulder, taking in her ponytail and yellow sundress. "Me, too. Western eggs okay for breakfast? Your fridge was nicely stocked with everything I needed."

She saw a stack of carefully folded clothing on one counter stool, including her bra, and sagged in relief. She'd forgotten about their wild, stripping dash from the barn to the house. What would Bender have thought if he'd walked into the barn and found her *underwear*?

"You're welcome." Rawlston had seen her eyeing the clothes. "I did a quick search when I got up. I think I found everything. Coffee's ready."

"Sounds divine." She slid onto a counter stool as he pushed a coffee mug across the island to her. "Wait, are we both morning people?"

"Looks that way. I think it comes with the territory when you're a rancher."

"Not necessarily," she said. "My sister Jade is non-functioning in the mornings."

He scooped the eggs onto two plates and joined her at the island. "But Jade's an accountant, right?"

She took a bite of her breakfast and moaned. "Oh, this is delicious. No, it's Sabrina who's an accountant. Jade's an animal-lover who wants to open a petting zoo on the ranch."

He chuckled. "Still, not the same as you and me. We have livestock to care for and a full day's hard labor waiting for us every morning."

She nodded, too busy enjoying breakfast to say anything. But she was thinking how nice it was to be with someone who understood. Not only understood, but *embraced* the same life that she did. Being outdoors all day. Worrying about the weather and the livestock. Spending hours on horseback. Backbreaking work that left a body aching and tired. She wouldn't trade it for anything, and she had a feeling Rawlston wouldn't, either.

They finished eating in an easy silence, then cleaned the kitchen together. She noticed he'd tossed a kitchen towel over the folder holding their annulment documents, and she decided to leave it there. She hadn't planned on springing those on him after last night, anyway. She was putting the clean dishes up in the cupboard when she felt his hands on her waist, gently pulling her back against his chest.

"What are we doing here, Dolly?"

"Oh my God, stop calling me that." It was automatic, but to be honest, she liked the sound of her hated nickname coming from him.

"You're avoiding the question, *Dahlia*." He brushed a light kiss against her neck. "What are we doing? Because I've gotta say, I'd like to keep doing it."

A warm glow washed over her. He wanted her—not just now, but ongoing. It was one more thing they had in common, because she wanted that, too. Even if she had no idea what that meant. For once, she didn't want to put her plans in a spreadsheet to be managed.

"Do we need to define it?" she asked quietly. "Can we just be two adults enjoying each other's company for now?"

He went still. "And how long is *for now* going to last?"

It was interesting that Mr. Laid-back was suddenly so concerned about getting all the details right, and she wasn't.

"Can we just take it day by day for now?"

"Again…what does *for now* mean?"

She turned in his embrace, sliding her arms around his waist. "Until one of us decides it's time to stop?"

He studied her face for a long beat, then nodded. He didn't look enthused, but she could tell he wasn't going to fight her on it. "I guess that works. I just… I don't want to share you. If we're together, we're together, period. I can handle temporary, but—"

"We're committed to each other while in our noncommittal relationship? That works for me." She reached up to cup his cheek. "I know we have a lot of stuff to figure out, but I want to enjoy this, *whatever* it is, for now."

"There are my favorite two words again." He grimaced. "But yes, I want us to be able to enjoy being together, too."

"And one more thing…" she started.

"Let me guess—we can't tell anyone."

She smiled. "Doesn't that make it more of an adventure?"

"Or a dirty little secret you're ashamed of."

"I'm not ashamed," she assured him. "Not of us. Not after last night. But…"

"But you don't want anyone to know…*for now*."

Chapter Fifteen

Rawlston strode into the LC Club Saturday night, feeling an uncharacteristic pulse of anticipation. Not just because of the annual summer reception for area ranchers
tonight. It was an event he'd come to enjoy, mainly because it was more casual than the ritzy cattlemen's Christmas ball in December. The summer reception was more
for mingling and laughter…and he didn't have to wear
a tuxedo. Sport coats were acceptable, and, while the
women certainly liked to dress up, it was more cocktail
or tea dresses than formal gowns.

He was happy to be there, but the anticipation he felt
was because of one person. Dahlia was going to be here,
along with the Fortune family. They'd made their plan
that morning—they'd arrive separately, mingle for half
an hour or so, and then bump into each other. Dahlia
reasoned that if they pretended to be surprised to see
each other, no one would suspect they'd been spending
their nights making love on pretty much every surface
in her house. And his.

Rawlston was doing his best to live in the moment,
rather than worrying about the time when *for now* would
come to an end. It wasn't hard to do when they were

naked together, focused only on pleasure. But during the day, when he was working his ranch and she was working hers, the worry crept in. She hadn't mentioned the annulment once since before their first night together, but that didn't mean she didn't still want one eventually. Meanwhile, he didn't want their marriage to end. Not yet…maybe not ever.

He entered the reception area, which took up the ballroom and a veranda overlooking Lake Chatelaine. He was scanning the crowd for a tall blonde when his father walked up to him, with JoAnn on his arm. This was her first time meeting all of the ranchers, and he thought she might be intimidated. After all, she'd come from a small Vermont dairy farm. At least, he'd assumed it was small, but he'd never asked. JoAnn looked totally at ease as she was introduced to people, though. She was wearing a softly shimmering purple pantsuit, with a long, loose jacket over a simple white top. Her pewter hair was pulled back into a twist.

It was a good reminder that he really needed to check his less-than-generous assumptions about the sturdily built farm woman. He was coming to like her, but he'd still assumed she'd look or feel out of place with the well-heeled LC Club crowd. Instead, she looked like she'd been here for years, cool and confident.

"Hey, son!" Keith Ames pulled Rawlston into an enthusiastic hug. "I was afraid you might have blown this off like you did last year."

"I was at my friend's wedding in Norfolk, Dad. I don't consider that *blowing off* the reception. I just had somewhere else to be that weekend. Hi, JoAnn. You look lovely."

"Thanks, Rawlston," she replied warmly. "You clean up pretty well yourself."

"You might want to keep that outfit handy for Thursday," his dad said, giving JoAnn a conspiratorial wink.

Rawlston couldn't think of anything going on that week. "What's happening on Thursday?"

"JoAnn and I are tying the knot down at the courthouse, and I'd like you to be our witness."

"*Already?*" He knew the word was a mistake as soon as he said it. His father glowered at him, and JoAnn looked anywhere but at Rawlston. "Look, I'm sorry for the way that came out. It's just happening…fast. But you two are very much adults, and it's your decision to make, not mine. I'm happy for you."

Was he also still a bit *concerned*? Heck yeah. But he tried to set that aside. JoAnn had given him absolutely no reason to doubt her sincerity. "I'd be honored to stand up for you, Dad."

His father beamed. "I was hoping you'd say that, son, because you were my only choice. Be there at two o'clock. We'll schedule a small reception at the house when her kids can get away to join us. Jo and I just wanted to make everything official. It's important to us."

Dad's look was a warning to Rawlston, and he rushed to assure them. "Of course. I understand." They were from a different generation, and they didn't want to *live in sin*.

Another group of cattle ranchers joined them, but the whole time he was chatting, he was searching the room for Dahlia. He spotted some of her siblings in the crowd, but not his wife. It wasn't a formal sit-down meal. Instead, it was what they called hot *hors d'oeuvres*, with food stations and bars scattered around the ballroom.

There were numerous tables, including taller café tables to stand at, and round dining tables with seating. A band was setting up on the far end of the room, near a small dance floor. But Dahlia was still nowhere to be found. He excused himself from the group gathered around his father. He had a feeling both the women and the men were curious to meet Keith Ames's new bride-to-be.

The Perry triplets were at one dining table, laughing with their spouses. He wondered if they'd learned any more about the mystery of possibly having a brother somewhere they'd never met. He caught a glimpse of long, blond hair across the room, and headed that way eagerly. It wasn't Dahlia, though. It was her mother, Wendy Fortune, who appeared to be deep in conversation with Beau Weatherly.

Looking at Wendy, it was easy to see where Dahlia and her sisters had gotten their tall, willowy good looks from. He'd only met their mom a few times before their move to Chatelaine. She had an aura about her that was intriguing. She was soft-spoken and kind, but he'd sensed there was an underlying strength to her as well. Maybe it was because she'd uprooted her life and her adult children to start fresh in Chatelaine. She'd embraced her newfound Fortune relatives, and the feeling was mutual. West Fortune had told Rawlston they all adored her.

Beau Weatherly saw Rawlston approaching, and stepped away from Wendy, apologizing to her for monopolizing her time with his stories. She laughed brightly, sounding just like Dahlia. Then she turned to Rawlston, and there was something in her gaze that said, *I know all about Vegas.* He held in a sigh. For someone who'd insisted on keeping the marriage and relationship top secret, Dahlia seemed to have spilled the truth to her whole family.

"Hi, Rawlston," Wendy said, extending her hand to him. "How lovely to see you, although I almost didn't recognize you out of your jeans and boots. You cut a fine figure, young man."

"And you look stunning, Wendy." He took her hand and gave a slight bow. She was in a flowing chiffon dress in a deep orange color with tiny yellow polka dots. It reminded him of something royalty might wear to a garden party. All she was missing was a wide-brimmed summer hat. "How are you liking your first rancher's reception?"

She glanced around the room before answering. "It's wonderful, but then I've thought that about everything I've experienced so far in Chatelaine."

"And how are the renovations coming at Fortune's Castle?" Dahlia had told him all about her mother's plans to convert the place into a venue.

She rolled her eyes and laughed again. "Right now, it's a dusty mess, but I can tell it's going to be beautiful when it's done. I've hired a marketing firm to start attracting customers." She glanced at Beau, who was standing nearby. "If you two gentlemen will excuse me, I'm going to go say hi to a friend I just spotted. Enjoy your evening!"

After she left, Beau gave Rawlston a searching look. The guy was sometimes downright spooky in the way he could read people. His expression went from one of curiosity to a knowing grin. *Damn.* Did he know, too? He couldn't imagine Dahlia telling him, though. He wasn't family.

"How're things going, Rawlston?" Beau took a glass

of bourbon from a server and drank from it. "Those Brahman cows doing okay for you? I've always favored the Herefords myself, but I heard the Brahmans handle our Texas summers well."

"Yes, sir, they're working out fine for me, and all is well in my world."

"I'll just bet it is," Beau answered.

Rawlston frowned. Maybe the guy *did* know something. Nevertheless, he was determined not to feed the gossip machine. "And how are things with you, Beau? I heard you're cutting back your herd a bit."

They talked for a few minutes about the challenges of raising beef cattle. Beau had sold off a portion of his herd, but he assured Rawlston he wasn't leaving ranching.

"It all still fascinates me," Beau confided. "Balancing the weather, the price of beef, the cost of raising cattle, getting good working horses to use on the range. I love ranching, but I'm reaching a stage of my life where I want to make time for other things."

Rawlston wondered what new endeavors the older man had in mind.

"You know," Beau continued, "I was just reading an interesting article on cattle ranching last week. All those wars that were fought over range space back in the eighteen and nineteen hundreds between cattlemen and sheep ranchers."

Rawlston worked to keep his face neutral as he nodded. What *did* the guy know? "Yes, I know about it. The sheep farmers came west, and the cattlemen didn't want the sheep ruining the range for their cattle."

He hadn't said much to Dahlia, but her sheep were regular trespassers onto his range. He'd started riding the fence line every day, looking for telltale tufts of wool, and then he'd send Tripp out to herd them back to her property. He was going to have to add a lower strand of wire to keep them on their side.

"That's just the thing," Beau said. "All that fighting was for nothing. Turns out sheep and cattle *can* graze the same range without a problem, as long as the population of each is properly balanced."

He had Rawlston's attention now. "That doesn't sound right. Sheep rip grass up by the roots and kill it."

Beau tipped his head to the side with a smile. "Now think about that, son. How could golf courses and parks use sheep to mow the lawns if they killed the grass they ate?"

Dahlia had said something similar that day when he'd been so cranky about finding her sheep with his cattle. If sheep killed grass, her range would be destroyed, and it wasn't. Beau was still talking.

"...turns out sheep have pretty sharp teeth, and they'll bite the grass off close to the ground, whereas cattle eat from the middle up. So it looks different, but they're not killing anything. Of course, if you have too many sheep mixed with cattle, the cattle will have less tall grass to eat. But with the right combination, the cattle chew the tops and make it easier for the sheep to graze, and the sheep eat it down to the ground, prompting new, healthy growth to start the cycle all over again. I can email you the article if you'd like."

"Yeah, sure," he answered, then caught himself. "Not that I'm planning on adding any sheep to my cattle herd, but it sounds interesting, if only for the sake of...science."

It wasn't the smoothest recovery, and Beau chuckled. "For science. *Right*. Because you've always been such a science guy." He leaned in close. "By the way, she's out on the veranda, wearing a pink dress that'll make your eyes pop."

Rawlston's pulse jumped. He didn't need to ask who Beau was talking about, and the older gentleman didn't need to explain. Giving up on pretending, he quickly excused himself and headed outside.

Dahlia was talking to her brother Ridge in a quiet corner of the veranda. *Lecturing* was more like it. She was concerned for her little brother and his big heart. The mysterious woman and her infant daughter were *still* living at his place, and he was still fiercely protective of them.

"Ridge, tell me the truth—is Evie actually your daughter or something? Did you have a relationship with that woman? Is this all some ruse to ease her into the family?"

He rolled his eyes dramatically. "As if I wouldn't be crowing from the rooftops if that beautiful baby girl was mine? Come on, Dahlia. Get real."

She pointed to herself. "Me? You want *me* to get real? You're the one possibly harboring a fugitive and her child at your *home*."

Ridge pulled her closer to the corner, with its spectacular views of the lake. He looked around, as if he thought the trees might be hiding spies. "Keep your voice down," he urged. "There are only a few people who know about Hope and Evie, and I want to keep it that way until she remembers more."

Dahlia tried to wrap her head around what her brother was doing. "But Hope isn't even her name!"

Ridge was annoyed. "What was I supposed to do—call her *Hey You*?"

She put her hand on his arm. "Honey, naming her is the least problematic thing you've done. I'm worried for you getting emotionally involved with this woman."

"*This woman* is intelligent, caring and frightened for her child's safety. What kind of man would I be if I didn't help her?" He stepped away from her touch, staring out at the water. "And it's not like I'm hiding her in a cave somewhere. The family knows she's there. My doctor friend knows she's there. I just don't want to go to the police yet, until we know more about what happened."

He turned to her. "What if Hope has some wacko husband who's trying to harm her, or kidnap Evie, or both? Have some faith in me, Dahlia." His expression brightened. "Why don't you stop over for lunch this week and meet her? It will make you feel better, and I think you'd like her. Oh, hi, Rawlston."

Her heart thumped in her chest, and it was all she could do not to spin with a bright smile to greet the man she'd been sleeping with for days now. Instead, she composed herself and turned slowly.

"Hi," she said, her voice deliberately cool. "It's good to see you." She stuck her hand out to Rawlston, and immediately regretted it. Her thought was that it would make them look like a pair of ranchers who barely knew each other. What she hadn't anticipated was that he would take her hand in his and hold it, with a wicked gleam in his eyes. His forefinger traced over the pulse point on her wrist, and her knees trembled under her long skirt. Rawlston's touch did that to her now. One fingertip on her skin could light her whole body up with red-hot desire. After holding her hand for what seemed like forever, he shook it formally.

"Why, Dahlia, what a pleasure. How are you and your family settling into Chatelaine?" The corner of his mouth twitched. She pulled her shoulders back and mirrored his movement, sliding her finger across the thin skin of his wrist. Two could play that game. The humor in his eyes turned to heat. *Touché.*

Ridge was babbling something about the ranch and the town and whatever, but she and Rawlston were locked in a moment meant only for them. There was no LC Club filled with ranchers. It was just him and her. He was taking in her dress, which she'd worn on purpose. They'd agreed to pretend to be acquaintances, but she hadn't been able to resist the body-skimming candy pink dress—the same color as the chapel in Las Vegas. The draped neckline was just low enough to be interesting, with tiny sleeves that draped off her shoulders. The hemline flared a bit, brushing her calves above white stilettos. She blinked, realizing they'd been silent too long. Ridge was staring at the two of them.

"Is everything okay between you guys? You *are* neighbors, you know." Oh, she knew. She knew that Rawlston rode Malloy to her ranch every evening, stabled him in the barn, and spent the nights with her with no one else being the wiser, then he'd ride his horse back to his place in the mornings. No telltale truck driving on or off the ranch to raise questions from Ridge or anyone else. She pulled her hand away and looked at her brother.

"We're having a bit of a range dispute, Ridge. My sheep are going through Rawlston's fence and he seems to think that's *my* problem. He's afraid my—what did you call them?—*fluffy squeak toys* will ruin the grazing for his precious cattle."

Ridge frowned. "Well, sheep can be a problem, sis. If they're trespassing on his land, technically he could shoot them."

She took a sharp breath. "He wouldn't dare!"

Rawlston gave her a lazy grin. "No, *he* wouldn't. And actually, I'm hearing it may not be as big a problem as I thought. I have more research to do on that. You look lovely tonight, Dahlia."

"Thank you." She did a mock curtsey, knowing she was giving him an extra special view of the dress's neckline. She wondered about his comment about the sheep, and made a mental note to ask him about it later. But tonight wasn't the right time. Haley Perry walked up to them, and Dahlia turned to greet her friend while Ridge and Rawlston talked cattle.

"That dress is stunning." Haley took Dahlia's hands and held her at arm's length, examining the dress. "That color suits you."

Dahlia caught Rawlston's eye. He was suppressing a grin at the comment. They both knew exactly why she'd worn that shade of pink—a color that hadn't been a big part of her wardrobe before.

"Thanks," she answered. "It was an impulse buy—I saw it and just had to have it, you know?"

Rawlston coughed, and she turned her back on him to avoid laughing. "How are things going with your search for your possibly-maybe brother?"

Haley shook her head sadly. "Nothing yet. We've submitted our DNA to two different companies, so if he does the same, we hope he'll reach out or that we'll find him." She shrugged. "*If* he exists, and *if* he wants to be found. The thing is, I have this really strong feeling that he's out there, and my sisters feel the same way. But I've checked every source I can think of, and there's no record of quads being born around our birth date. That doesn't make it impossible, though. As you've learned, the Fortunes are full of secrets, surprises and mysteries, and I guess that goes for anyone who marries into the family."

The two women chatted a bit longer, then Haley went off to greet someone else and Ridge left, probably rushing home to Hope and Evie. Rawlston was gone, too, but she quickly spotted him heading back her way, two drinks in hand. He gave her one, and they walked back into the ballroom, where the band had begun to play. She told him what Haley had said about "secrets, surprises and mysteries" and he'd agreed.

"From what I've discovered, she's spot-on. The Fortune name seems to attract drama." He smirked at her. "That explains a lot, actually."

She gave him a light smack on the arm, making him laugh. This was uncharted territory for her—a relationship filled with laughter, fun and complete acceptance of one another. It was new yet, but still, he supported her choices, even when he didn't understand them. He said they were her decisions to make. She couldn't remember *any* man in her life ever saying that to her. They'd either blatantly told her she was making bad choices— like her father—or had quietly manipulated and gaslighted her toward doing what *they* wanted her to do. Rawlston made her feel secure in being herself. It was a very nice feeling to have.

They stood together quietly and watched as couples

danced to a hip-hop tune. There was another fast song, and then the band slowed with a cover of Ed Sheeran's "Perfect." Rawlston took the glass from her hand and set it next to his on a nearby table, then led her to the dance floor. She started to resist. This was very public, and people might get the wrong idea about them. Or…the *right* idea, but one they'd agreed to keep secret for now.

Fortunes and their secrets.

Rawlston raised one eyebrow, waiting for her to decide what to do. The fact that he left it up to her, without pressure, was what propelled her into his arms. And just like that, they were dancing for the very first time together. Like everything else they did, it felt as if they'd done it all their lives. Easy. Comfortable. Requiring no effort as they glided across the dance floor. Her hand on his shoulder, his hand on her hip. Their eyes locked on each other and nowhere else. They started at a respectable distance apart, but by the time the chorus began, they were pressed against each other, drawn like magnets to be touching in every possible way. He twirled her gently, then dipped her deep at the end of the song.

Was anyone else dancing? She couldn't say. Was anyone else even in the ballroom? She didn't care. He straightened and she stayed in the hold of his arms, so strong and sure. And in that moment, brief as a heartbeat, she fell in love with Rawlston Ames.

The band started a line dance and the floor soon crowded with people. She and Rawlston went back to their drinks, as if nothing had changed. As if she hadn't been shaken to the core by doing the last thing she'd expected or even imagined possible.

Dahlia had fallen for her husband.

Chapter Sixteen

Rawlston stood outside the Chatelaine courthouse and watched as his wife strolled toward him on the sidewalk from where she'd parked, a block away. She was in one of her flowy skirts and ruffled blouses, with flat sandals. Dressy, but not overly so. Her hair was straight and free, the way she knew he liked it. She looked perfect. As usual.

He'd been surprised how easy it was to convince Dahlia to join him at his father's courthouse wedding. After they'd danced at the reception, close and intimate, she'd seemed preoccupied and quiet. Not upset, just a little withdrawn. She'd told him nothing was wrong when he asked, but something was going on with her. He hoped it wasn't regret, because he'd hate to see their relationship end.

It was pretty funny, actually. He was the one determined to avoid relationships, and now he was fretting that *she* might choose to walk away. They'd agreed not to define what they had. Not to make it permanent. Just keep it day-to-day. *For now*, as she'd said over and over. Until one of them decided to end it. He'd been okay with that then. Not thrilled, but okay. Every night they spent together made it much less okay.

His horse knew the ride to Dahlia's place by heart now.

Every evening, he'd saddle up and head her way. Every morning, he'd saddle up and ride home. And every day, it got harder and harder to leave her. To play their little game of not telling anyone. She'd told him what Haley said about Fortunes having secrets, surprises and mysteries.

He and Dahlia had the *secret* part down. The *surprise* was how much he wanted what they had to be permanent. The *mystery* was how she'd managed to change his mind about relationships and…maybe even marriage. That last one was tricky. Maybe she was changing his mind, or maybe he was conflicted because of his father's sudden dive into this wedding of his.

"I'm getting used to seeing you in suits." Dahlia stopped at his side with a bright smile. "It's a good look." She nodded toward the courthouse steps. "Are you ready for this?"

"I don't think Dad cares if I'm ready. It's *his* wedding."

"You know what I mean," she answered, putting her arm through his. "Have you accepted it, in your heart?" She patted his chest. It was a surprising show of affection in the middle of town on a sunny late-August afternoon. She seemed to come to the same conclusion, stepping back and releasing his arm. "I forgot, we're just friends. How *did* you explain my presence here to your father and JoAnn?"

He grimaced. "I…uh…didn't."

Her eyes went round. "Oh my God, you didn't tell them I'm coming? I'd better wait out here—"

"No! Look, you asked how I'm dealing with this, and the truth is, I'm still struggling. I need you here. I trust you to keep me from doing or saying something stupid."

Her eyes softened, making his chest feel warm. He

loved it when she let down her guard with him. It felt like a gift, and she'd been doing it more and more lately.

"I'm happy to help, but what do we say when your dad sees me with you?"

"Nothing. He…uh…he knows. I'm guessing JoAnn does, too."

She hesitated, and he thought she was going to blast him for telling anyone. But then she shrugged. "Okay. Let's go, then."

"You're not angry?"

"I told two of my sisters and my mom. I can hardly fault you for telling *one* family member. Come on, we shouldn't keep them waiting."

He wasn't sure who this new, mellow Dahlia was, but she was nice to be around.

The wedding was quick and charming. Dad was in his best suit. JoAnn wore a pale blue lace dress and carried a small bouquet of black-eyed Susans. They were beaming at each other, and Rawlston found himself smiling, too. He hadn't seen his father this genuinely happy in years. If JoAnn could do that, then he would welcome her to the family wholeheartedly. Neither seemed surprised to see Dahlia with Rawlston, and they'd warmly welcomed her as their second witness.

They were leaving immediately for Boston, where his father would meet his bride's family. Rawlston wondered what they'd think about meeting him *after* the wedding, but JoAnn had insisted they only wanted her to be happy. Dad was taking JoAnn to Europe in the fall for the official honeymoon.

And just like that, in less than an hour, he and Dahlia

were standing together on the sidewalk again, waving goodbye to his father and JoAnn—his new stepmother.

"This is weird," he said as their car drove away. "I'm okay with it, but it's still weird."

She touched his side lightly, not wanting to make a public spectacle. The brief touch was enough to let him know she cared, but, as always, it left him wanting more.

"This all happened pretty quickly. Why don't you come to the house early today? We can take a ride together before dinner to clear your head."

He nodded as they started walking. "A lot of things are happening quickly lately."

"I know. It's been one thing after another for you and me both." She gave him a strange sideways glance. "But that's not always a bad thing, is it? Sometimes surprises can turn out pretty well."

There was more meaning to her words than she was letting on…and he was about to ask for an explanation when a tall, blond-haired man walked up in front of them. Rawlston bristled, stepping ahead of Dahlia, but, being Dahlia, she shoved him to the side.

"Sorry to bother you," the man said, "but I'm new here and I'm looking for someone. Do either of you know a woman with the last name Perry? Actually, I think there's three women here who might have that name." He must have seen the caution on both of their faces, because he held his hands up in innocence. "I'm Heath Blackwood. I promise I'm not here to cause any trouble. I just have…business with the Perrys."

Rawlston started to tell the guy to get lost, but Dahlia put her hand on his arm to stop him. She was studying

Heath intently, then she smiled and took the hand he'd held out.

"Hi, Heath." She introduced herself and Rawlston. The usually cynical Miss Fortune was Miss Chatty all of a sudden. "All three of the Perry triplets live in the area, but they don't have the last name *Perry* anymore. One of them is a good friend of mine." She checked her watch. "I'm sure you'll find Haley Perry at the newspaper office this time of day." She gave him directions and sent him on his way.

Before Rawlston could ask what was going on, she turned to him, excitement written on her face. "Did you see his eyes? Just like the triplets'! I think he might be the Perry's mystery brother."

"Wait. The triplets are actually quads?" He was confused. "I've heard his name before, but it was about business, not the Perrys." Rawlston was pretty sure Blackwood did something in tech. "His *business* with them is probably just that."

Dahlia wasn't convinced. "Maybe. They're not sure a brother even exists. But there is a rumor and they're trying to track it down."

She told him about the hazy claim that there'd been a boy, possibly born with the girls, or possibly not. Rawlston couldn't deny a family resemblance, but the odds that Blackwood was that long-lost sibling were mighty low. He didn't want to diminish Dahlia's enthusiasm though. It was a wild story, but then again, things had been wild around Chatelaine for a while now. He looked at this tall, caring, incredible woman in front of him.

Ever since Dahlia Windham Fortune *Ames* came to town.

* * *

Dahlia stared at her twin in shock. "You got the same invitation?"

They were sitting on the veranda at Fortune's castle, staring at the two embossed ivory wedding invitations sitting on the table. She'd come to ask their mother if she knew anything about the strange invitation, but she wasn't there. The young woman at the front desk—the spa was having a soft opening that week—said Wendy Fortune was going to be spending a few days in San Antonio, visiting a spa that was owned by a friend there.

Just as Dahlia had turned to leave, Sabrina walked up the steps to the castle, so they'd decided to have a glass of tea together. She'd told Sabrina about the invitation, putting hers on the table, and Sabrina had pulled out an identical invitation.

The gold-stamped invitations read:

> *You are cordially invited to attend*
> *a very special wedding*
> *to be held at the Chatelaine Courthouse.*
> *More details will follow, but please*
> *save the date.*
> *You won't want to miss it!*

Sabrina tapped her invitation. "The date is in January, but it says nothing about who is getting married. And it's not just you and me. We *all* got them—Jade, Ridge, Arlo and Nash. I don't know, maybe the whole town got them. Maybe it's some sort of annual Chatelaine ritual or a PR trick for some company."

Dahlia shrugged. "I was going to ask Mom if she might have heard something about it. You know how plugged in she is with what's happening in Chatelaine. She has her fingers on all the gossip."

Sabrina snorted. "That's exactly why I drove over. But she's not answering her phone."

"I guess she's on a business trip to San Antonio, so that might be why she's not answering. Something about a friend who owns a spa there?"

Sabrina thought for a moment. "She did mention a college classmate who has some sort of day spa. It could be in San Antonio." She slumped back in her chair. "Well, damn. Who's going to give us the gossip now?"

They laughed, and changed the subject, tucking the mystery invitations in their bags. Sabrina was right— it was probably something silly like a publicity stunt.

She stopped at GreatStore to pick up some groceries for dinner that night. Rawlston was coming over, of course, but tonight would be different. Tonight she was going to tell him she loved him. That he made her feel the way no other man had made her feel. Respected. Accepted. Cherished. Possibly even…loved?

She suspected he felt the same way she did, but he hadn't said anything. Maybe because of all her rules to keep things casual, where either one of them could just walk away without a word. At the time, she'd thought it best. But she'd had no idea she was going to fall in love with the man.

"Dahlia!" A woman's voice called out from behind her. She turned to see Haley, her cart loaded to overflowing with baby food and paper products. Her friend gestured at the cart. "Sure, you're carrying everything in a basket, and I'm going to need a second cart pretty soon! I'm helping Tabitha and West restock. Their twins both have tummy bugs, and everyone in that house is exhausted. What do you have in there?" She peeked in the basket, then started to laugh. "If I didn't know better, I'd say that's a date night in the making. Shrimp, steaks, veggies, wine and…oh, is that tiramisu cake?"

Dahlia froze. "Just…um…a friend coming into town from Dallas." She forced a laugh. "Nothing scandalous, I promise."

It wasn't a lie. There was nothing scandalous about her having dinner with her husband. And telling him how much she loved him. She suddenly remembered crossing paths with the man in town who looked so much like Haley.

"Oh! How did your meeting go the other day with that guy?" She couldn't remember his name off the top of her head. "I sent him to the office."

Haley stared at her blankly. "What guy?"

"His name was Heath. He didn't…?" She stopped. If Blackwood didn't introduce himself to Haley, he may have had a good reason. Maybe Rawlston had been right, and Heath was just here on business. Perhaps Haley hadn't been there, or he'd talked to Tabitha or Lily instead. Or maybe she'd spoil his surprise if she said any more. All she knew for sure was that this was one Fortune family drama she didn't need to be in the middle of. "Oh, never mind. I must have misunderstood. When did the twins get sick…?"

She and Haley chatted for a few more minutes, then she headed toward checkout. Her nerves were jumping with anticipation of tonight with Rawlston. She didn't know how he would react to her confession of love, but there was no way she could hold it inside any longer.

Chapter Seventeen

"So your dad and JoAnn get back from their honeymoon tomorrow?" Dahlia set a glass of dark beer by Rawlston's seat. They were on the deck, watching the sun set low over the lake. He took the beer with a nod of thanks. He enjoyed their evenings out here, after a nice meal as the air began to cool.

Who was he kidding? He enjoyed any time he spent with Dahlia. In fact, he was beginning to despise any time he spent *away* from her. His world had shifted to revolve around his wife. And that was okay. Which was the biggest surprise of all. He was not only okay with it, he was loving it. Loving *her*. Things were great between them. They spent nearly every night together, usually at her place. They'd fallen into an easy routine around each other. It was comfortable. Which had him feeling suddenly vulnerable.

"Yeah," he answered. "It wasn't really a honeymoon, though. Just a quick trip to meet her children. Dad said it went well."

He'd spoken to his father a few hours ago, and it sounded as though their trip to Boston to meet JoAnn's family had been a success. They'd been introduced over brunch on the first day there, and were all going to a nice seafood restaurant tonight before Dad and JoAnn headed back to Texas.

Dahlia sat next to him on the upholstered outdoor sectional, her wineglass in her hand. "Remember what I said…"

"I know, I know. It's a marriage, whether it happens in a judge's chambers, a church or…" he winked at her "…a Vegas chapel."

It was a risk, bringing that up. They'd *both* stopped mentioning the wedding or their current state of matrimony. But they couldn't ignore it forever. They were legally husband and wife. The annulment papers were sitting in a folder on the kitchen island, but she hadn't mentioned them once since they'd started sleeping together. Maybe she didn't want the annulment anymore. Or was she thinking this was just a fling between them?

Dahlia had gone still at his side, her glass in her hand, staring out across the water. She finally took a sip, and he had a feeling she was measuring her words carefully.

"Yes, it's a marriage no matter what. And the location doesn't determine the success of that marriage. I think your dad and JoAnn are going to be good together. They seem to truly care for each other, you know?"

So she was still avoiding the topic of *their* marriage. He went along with it.

"I guess so. I'm still not sure why they needed to make it official so quickly, but Dad said they were both determined not to just live together. As if that's so bad. Everyone does it these days. I don't think there'd be any scandal about it."

"I've never thought of your dad as the old-fashioned type, to be worried about that. But I don't know about

JoAnn." She moved in closer to his side, and he slid his arm around her shoulder. She looked up at him. "I think being married shows how committed they are to the relationship."

"Being married is just a piece of paper, Dolly. We're living proof of that."

There. He'd thrown the topic of their marriage out there again. She blinked and looked away.

"Keith and JoAnn didn't get drunk and wander into a wedding chapel," she said. "They made a conscious decision to commit to their love for each other. I know Lana burned you, but you can't possibly think *all* marriages are bad because of that one experience. Your parents were happily married for decades."

He considered that for a moment as he drank his beer.

"Don't you think people learn the most from their own experience?" he asked. "Sure, I've observed people being happy in a marriage, but just because I've seen my dad fly a plane doesn't mean I know to fly one. Maybe the issue is that I don't think *I'm* cut out for a successful marriage, because I haven't experienced one."

"Well, that's just…sad." She sighed, resting her head on his shoulder. "Have you given up all hope, then?"

"I don't know about *all* hope, but I've been highly skeptical about the idea."

Except with her. He might have some hope of happiness in a marriage with Dahlia. A *real* marriage. He frowned, yearning for something more than what they had now, with both of them refusing to talk about what was next. It didn't have to be tonight, but sooner or later, they were going to have to discuss their future.

He'd seen Arlo Fortune yesterday at the feedstore, and

Dahlia's brother had mentioned that Carter Powers was due back any day now. Carter was another one of those topics that had been carefully avoided between Dahlia and Rawlston. And he sure as hell wasn't going to bring that one up. He rested his cheek on the top of her head.

They stayed like that, relaxed and snuggled together, for a while, watching the Texas sky turn shades of coral and pink, then deep purple as the sun disappeared below the horizon. They both sipped from their drinks, content to just…be. Then Dahlia gave a quick laugh, sitting up to look at him, her eyes bright with humor.

"What?" he asked, smiling in return.

"It's so ironic that you have all these feelings about the institution of marriage, but I couldn't convince you to end ours, no matter how hard I tried. Why were you so stubborn about it?"

She hadn't mentioned if she *still* wanted to end the marriage. She was talking about it being a thing of the past. But more importantly, she was point-blank asking him why he'd stalled the annulment. And he couldn't lie to her anymore.

He hesitated long enough that Dahlia noticed. But her smile was still in place as she playfully nudged his ribs with her elbow.

"Seriously, what made you so determined to avoid it? I never did believe your 'lucky pen' story, and I know you spilled that tea on purpose. You probably fibbed about your printer, too, right?"

He nodded, wishing he didn't have to tell her, but knowing he had no choice. Dahlia's smile began to fade as she studied his face.

"Rawlston?"

"Look," he started, trying to think of a way to soften the blow. But he knew her so much better now. She was fiercely self-reliant, and she probably wasn't going to appreciate his good intentions. "Every time I thought about you being with Carter Powers, it just…frustrated me."

Her forehead furrowed. "You were jealous?"

"What? God, no!" Not at the time, anyway. He hadn't known then that she would steal his heart and own his soul. "But he's…he's not who you think he is, Dahlia. You deserve so much better than a sleazeball like Carter."

She sat up straighter, shrugged out of his embrace.

"Yes." She spoke carefully. "I agree with you. But what did Carter have to do with you not signing the annulment? You've made it pretty clear you don't believe in marriage."

"I don't. At least… I didn't. It's not like we intended to end up married to each other. But you'd said something about Carter proposing to you when he came back from his trip, and—" He paused. Had she just agreed that she deserved better than Carter? So maybe he didn't need to confess… *No.* If there was any chance of a forever between Dahlia and him, he had to tell her the truth. "You said yourself you couldn't do that if we were legally married. I wanted you to have time to see him for who he really is. The guy isn't just ambitious, Dahlia. He's unethical—he doesn't care who he hurts to get what he wants. He cost my dad nearly a quarter million dollars in one of his schemes."

There was a long beat of heavy silence before Dahlia stood and began to pace back and forth on the deck. Even then, it was a while before she spoke.

"So let me understand this…" Her words were slow

and deliberate, and she wouldn't even look at him. He had a feeling this was very bad. She paced some more. "You didn't sign the annulment papers because you wanted to block me from marrying Carter...by forcing me to remain married to you."

"*Forcing* is putting it harshly, I think."

She came to an abrupt halt, staring at him in disbelief. "Tell me how I'm wrong, Rawlston. You made every excuse not to sign. I thought maybe it was something cute, like...you *liked* me, or something."

He more than liked her. He was in love with the furious woman standing in front of him, hands resting on her hips, clenched into tight, angry fists.

"Dahlia, I *do* li—"

"Eh-eh!" She held up one hand, opening then pinching her thumb and fingers together in the universal signal to shut the hell up. "Didn't you just tell me you didn't sign because you didn't want me to marry Carter?"

"Well—"

"Never mind. I know what you said. You didn't talk to me about it. You didn't say, *Hey, you might want to rethink your plans and here's why.* You never told me your dad lost all that money with Carter. You just manipulated me to keep me from doing something you thought I wanted to do."

She'd nailed it, laying out exactly what he'd done. He had no defense, but he had to try.

"I know it sounds bad, but I really was trying to protect you."

"From what? My own judgment? You knew better than me, huh? I... God, I can't even look at you right now." She spun to stare out at the darkening lake. "You should go."

He stood and walked up behind her, knowing better than to touch her. "Dahlia, I'm sorry. I told Jade it was a bad idea—"

Her shoulders went even stiffer. "This was my *sister's* idea?"

"No! No, I swear this is all on me. But she said you'd told her about Vegas, and she...supported my plan." He had a feeling he'd just made things worse by mentioning Jade. He was still speaking to Dahlia's back, talking faster to say as much as possible before she forced him to leave. "It was a stupid idea. At first it was more about Carter. He's a jackass who doesn't deserve you. And then...then we spent more time together and I started falling for you. I hated the thought of you being with him. And then..."

He gently rested his hands on her shoulders. She didn't relax into his touch the way she usually did, but she didn't pull away, either. "And then we kissed, and made love, and I was in too deep, babe. It became all about me not wanting to lose you—to him or anyone else. *Ever.* And as you and I became more serious, I didn't know how to explain all of this to you—"

She turned and faced him, her large eyes shining with tears. It felt like a razor blade was being run across his heart.

"You should have told me the truth."

"I just *did* tell you the truth, and I've gotta be honest—this is not going all that great for me." If he'd hoped his attempt at lightness would help, he was wrong. Her eyes narrowed.

"It hasn't been great for me, either. It's bad enough that you thought you had the right to manipulate me and keep me from making a decision about Carter *myself.* That's worse than bad, actually. It's...downright awful. But then, even after we started being..." she gestured vaguely "... I don't know—intimate? Serious? In a relationship? What *have* we been doing?" She pulled away from him, as if she could no longer tolerate his touch. "Whatever it was, I damn sure deserved to know the truth a lot sooner than this. How am I supposed to trust you now, Rawlston?"

She stomped toward the house, and he followed automatically. He wasn't sure how he was able to move, because he'd felt his heart stop when she said she couldn't trust him. She headed for the front of the house, ushering him out of her home, and possibly out of her life. He had no idea how to defend himself without making things even worse. Dahlia stopped near the front door, and gave a bitter, humorless laugh.

"My sisters didn't want me with Carter because they said he was so much like our father. But *you're* the one who tried to gaslight me, which is *exactly* what Dad would do when he didn't like my decisions. So, really, what is the difference between the two of you?"

"The difference is I love you." Saying it wasn't planned, but she needed to know it. "You wanted the truth, and that's it. I love you, Dahlia."

She tried to corral her emotions, but they refused to be tamed. This whole conversation had spun out of control, and now he was saying *this*? Did he think she was going to just forget everything else? Forget that he'd lied to her? Manipulated her? And worse…tried to take away her ability to make her own decisions?

"Seriously? You think *now* is the time to tell me you love me?" She folded her arms on her chest, mainly to keep him from seeing how her hands were trembling. "How am I supposed to believe you?"

"Look, I screwed up. It was a stupid plan I cooked up weeks ago. I didn't know what would happen between us. I didn't know I was going to fall madly in love with you." He put his hands on her shoulders, but she quickly pulled away, shaking her head to warn him not to try that again. His hands fell to his sides. "Yes, I made up a few stories about lucky pens and my printer not working. It was bad, but I swear on my mother's grave those are the only lies I've told. Everything else between us has been genuine. Including my love—"

"Stop *saying* that!" Her raised voice echoed off the walls. His claims of loving her hurt more than his duplicity about their annulment. "Saying *I love you* isn't a get-out-of-jail-free card. The more you insist on saying it, the more I wonder about the convenient timing of this sudden revelation." Why did he look so confused? How could he not get this? "Rawlston, I don't believe you. I don't know if I'll ever believe you again. You didn't trust me to make the right choice about Carter, so you played games with my heart… Hell, you played games with the rest of my *life*."

He jammed his fingers through his hair, his face going red. "Damn it to hell, Dolly, if you think I'm the kind of man who would toss around the L-word lightly, you don't know me at all."

"I didn't think you'd lie to me, either," she answered hotly. "But here we are. I clearly *don't* know you."

"I'm the same man that you made love to last night!" His volume rose. "I'm the guy you ride with. The guy you dine with. The man who held you in his arms by the firepit and listened to all the crap your dad did, and the man who understood why you still mourned his death."

That had happened two nights ago. She'd had a bout of melancholy over her father's death and their complicated relationship. How she'd spent her teen years working so hard to please him, and then her adult years blatantly defying every so-called *suggestion* Dad had for her life—personally and professionally. She and her father hadn't argued as much as they'd continually danced around his constant disappointment in her and her quiet but determined defiance of him. And yet...

Her father was dead. And since his death, it sometimes felt as if the family was rushing headlong to change *everything* about their lives. Moving to Chatelaine. Changing jobs. Changing *names*. The experience sometimes left her feeling conflicted. The man had never seemed satisfied with her, but she still mourned his loss. It was confusing and frustrating.

That had been when Rawlston had moved over to her chaise by the firepit and pulled her onto his lap, holding her like a child against his chest while she'd cried. He'd whispered words of comfort to her, telling her that nothing she was feeling was wrong. That it was natural, and she should embrace her feelings instead of bottling them up. God, how she'd wept at that. How she'd *loved* this man.

But her anger burned bright and hot right now. Perhaps even more so. Him being so good then made his betrayal all the worse.

"This isn't a negotiation. You can't pay off your mistakes by listing good things you've done. It doesn't erase anything. You *hurt* me, Rawlston." She put her hand over her heart. "I can't… I can't deal with you right now. Please go."

He looked as shattered as she felt, but she didn't have it in her to feel sympathetic. The pain was too sharp and hot. His eyes glistened with unshed tears.

"Dahlia, the last thing I wanted was to hurt you." His voice cracked with emotion. "I'll do whatever you want. You want the papers signed? I'll do it. I'll give you whatever you want."

Chapter Eighteen

"**W**ait." Jade leaned forward to take Dahlia's hand. "He *signed* the annulment papers? Just like that?"

"It was *his* idea." Dahlia sniffed, trying to stop crying after doing it for three long nights. How could she miss someone she was so damn *mad* at?

"It sounds like he was desperate, sis." Sabrina was next to Jade. They were on the veranda at Fortune's Castle. Their mother was sitting at Dahlia's side, but she hadn't said much yet.

"Of course he was desperate," Dahlia snapped. "He did the one thing that's a deal breaker for me—he tried to make a decision *for* me."

"But it was the *right* decision," Jade pointed out. "Even you agree that Carter was all wrong for you. God, I wish I could have been a fly on the wall, or on a tree, for that wedding proposal. Did Carter really have an arbor of yellow roses in the shape of Texas?"

Dahlia buried her face in her hands. "Don't remind me. I tried to stop him, but he wouldn't listen. I said we needed to talk, and he insisted we were 'late' and had to get to the park. I should have just sent him a Dear John email two weeks ago, but I felt like I owed him an explanation in person. Just like everything else this week, it was a disaster."

She and Carter had arrived at the historic gardens outside Austin two days ago. Carter had led her to a giant, rose-covered arbor in the shape of Texas, with the sun setting behind them, making the roses glow. It was lovely, but as usual with Carter, it was...too much. The thing had to be seven feet high, and had a banner on top that spelled out T-e-x-a-s, just in case anyone was confused. It was more appropriate for a campaign photo than a proposal setting.

When she'd spotted the photographer setting up a tripod, she'd realized that's exactly what Carter intended. He was planning to use their engagement in his political campaign. *Look at me, I married a pretty blonde Fortune girl from Texas!* She'd dug her heels in and physically tried to stop him, but he'd had her hand in his and would not slow down. He muttered something about "don't be nervous" and "we're losing the light," never thinking she was about to dump him. On camera.

The one blessing was that the cameraman was the only witness, hired by Carter. He had staged this to *look* intimate and private...but conveniently captured on film by a professional photographer to be shared later. Carter had dropped to one knee and opened that box to display an enormous diamond-encrusted ring, with a three-carat round diamond set high above the rest. It was gaudy and completely impractical for a rancher like her.

All she could think about as she stared at the ring was the one Rawlston had given her in Vegas. Their gold and platinum wedding bands had matched, but he'd bought her a diamond, too. A simple square pillow cut stone in a low gold setting that would protect it. It had been perfect for her. And she'd made him return it the next morning.

She'd turned Carter down as gently as possible, aware of the photographer videotaping every word. She told him she didn't love him, and wouldn't pretend to in order to help his campaign. The truth was, she didn't want to be a politician's wife. Didn't want to live in Austin. Didn't want to marry him. She wanted to raise sheep in Chatelaine. With Rawlston...but she didn't say that last bit to Carter. No need to rub salt in the wound. Besides, a future with Rawlston was highly in doubt right now. They hadn't spoken in days, and she was still working through her feelings about what he'd done.

Carter had been stunned at first, then quickly angry. After sending the photographer away, he'd told Dahlia how she'd humiliated him, how she was making the "biggest mistake of her life," how much she'd regret it one day. She'd let him rant, knowing he was already recalculating a solution in his mind. After he'd settled down, he gave her one last, dismissive look.

"It's just as well. You'd have made a lousy campaign wife anyway. You'd rather chase around after a bunch of stupid sheep." He'd turned away. "You'll end up married to some dirt-poor rancher, watching me on television and wondering where it all went wrong."

She hadn't answered, letting him walk away and leave her there in front of the giant rose map of Texas. She'd gone from two men in her life to none. But at least *she'd* controlled both situations. She turned to Jade.

"Yes, I realized Carter was wrong for me," she answered. "But *I* decided that, for *myself.* It wasn't Rawlston's choice to make. And it wasn't *yours*, either. I can't believe you encouraged him."

"Because I *care*," Jade replied. "Sometimes you get so bullheaded that you refuse to listen to anyone, even if they're trying to help. You met a guy just like Dad, one you know Dad would have approved of, and you dug your heels in." Jade squeezed her hands. "You define the phrase 'cut off your nose to spite your face,' girl. We thought if Rawlston could give you some time to slow your roll, it would just…help you make your own decision. We weren't trying to make it *for* you."

Wendy Fortune shook her head with a sad smile. "I love you, my darling daughters, but what you two and Rawlston did to your sister was wrong. Well-intentioned? Yes. But wrong."

"Thank you, Mom." Dahlia pulled her hands from Jade's, but she did it gently. Her hot rage from the other night had faded to a dull hurt and sadness that weighed on her.

"Don't thank me yet, young lady." Mom turned to face her. "Because Jade is right—sometimes making your *own* choice is more important to you than making the *right* choice."

"But—"

"I'm not finished," Mom interrupted. "I *love* you, Dahlia. I love your fierceness and your independence. They are gifts that make you uniquely you. But sometimes you hide behind them to protect yourself, and you end up missing out. The question is, are you doing that now?"

"I…" Dahlia slumped back in her chair. "I don't know, Mom. Rawlston really hurt me. He lied to me. How am I supposed to forgive that?"

"Do you love him?"

"Yes." She didn't hesitate with her answer. "And I miss him. Everything feels all wrong without him in my life. But what he *did* was wrong, too."

Sabrina sighed. "It sounds like you're trying to do my thing, creating some sort of balance sheet to sum up what he did versus what you did and what he'd have to do to make you 'even' or something. I'm no expert—" Sabrina laughed softly "—but I don't think that's how relationships work. You're two humans, which means you're both going to screw up. One of you will be right and the other will be wrong, or maybe—just maybe— you'll *both* be wrong. Like now."

Dahlia bristled. "How are we *both* wrong? He lied. He manipulated. He signed the damn annulment papers."

"Honey," Jade said, "he lied about having a lucky pen. It's not like he lied about hiding some secret love child or something scandalous like that. And yes, I see why you say he manipulated you, but…that started before you two were in a relationship."

"We were *married*."

"Give me a break," Sabrina scoffed. "You stumbled into a chapel while drunk and you didn't even remember it the next morning. That is *not* a relationship. The relationship came after you got back to Chatelaine. And he didn't lock you in a basement somewhere. He just didn't sign the paperwork."

"Until he *did* sign it."

Sabrina threw her hands up in frustration. "Because that's what you'd wanted all along! You can't be mad at him for *not* signing *and* for signing."

"Girls." Their mother's voice was soft but firm.

"We've all had a chance to share our views about Rawlston, but your sister needs to make this decision on her own." She spoke directly to Dahlia. "You said you love him, and I believe you. He told you he loves you, too, and I think that's true. Love has a way of sneaking up on you like that, out of the blue. And when it does, you have to grab it." Mom paused, a soft smile appearing and quickly disappearing again. "You're hurt and angry right now, but are you willing to give him up forever? Or are you willing to forgive him? You two had an unconventional start, but that doesn't mean you don't have a path forward if you're willing to work at it. Have you talked at all?"

Dahlia shook her head. Rawlston had certainly tried. He'd called and texted over and over, begging forgiveness. Asking to talk. He'd even come to the ranch, but Sabrina had sent him home at Dahlia's request. She furrowed her brow, remembering how he'd left a voicemail just that morning. His voice had sounded muffled, as if he'd been drinking. But that couldn't be, not at that hour.

She wanted to forgive him, but she was afraid. Dahlia had thought he was the one guy who was different from other men in her life. She'd thought he was her safe place. That she could trust him. What he did, and the fact that he hadn't told her, had shaken that trust.

Wendy Fortune sat up, checking her watch. "I'm sorry, but I have a potential corporate client coming in to tour the castle as a possible work retreat location. I'll call you later, sweetheart." Their mother stood and kissed each of them, staying longer over Dahlia, before heading back inside. There was a beat of silence around the table.

"So..." Jade began. "Any more news on those wedding invitations?"

Sabrina embraced the topic change with a loud, animated laugh. "No! And it's making me crazy. The invitations were expensive, so I guess that's a clue, but not much of one. Dahlia, do you have any ideas?"

She knew what they were doing—distracting her from Rawlston. She smiled. It was a little shaky, but it was her first in a few days. And that gave her just a glimmer of hope. She was going to get through this, no matter what happened. Because she had a family who would always be there for her. She gave them an exaggerated shrug, with her hands in the air.

"I've got nothing. I asked Haley if there'd ever been a mysterious event like this in Chatelaine before, but she doesn't know any more than we do." She couldn't help herself. "It must be nice to be able to plan a wedding instead of waking up married to a guy who won't even fight to keep you."

"Technically, Rawlston *did* fight to keep you by not signing the annulment," Sabrina pointed out. "But Mom wants us to keep our opinions to ourselves so that you can do this on your own, so forget I said anything." She made a motion with her hand as if locking her lips with a key. "You're on your own, twinsie."

And that was the problem.

Bottom line? She had to listen to her heart. And her heart was telling her that Rawlston was still her safe place.

Rawlston knocked back a shot of whiskey on the patio behind his house. It was ten o'clock in the morning, but he figured the drink was medicinal. If you wanted to cure a hangover, you were supposed to drink something, right? Hair of the dog and all that. He grabbed the bottle at his side and refilled the shot glass. At least he wasn't drinking straight from the bottle, like he'd done the first couple of days.

It wasn't like him to drown his sorrows. But he'd never had a sorrow this deep before. A sorrow he couldn't see a way out of. And a love that apparently wasn't returned. Or that had been shattered by his foolish attempt to protect her. He downed another shot with a grimace. The whiskey wasn't hitting his empty stomach well at all.

Dahlia hadn't needed his so-called protection. As much as he wanted to deny it, the real reason he'd delayed signing those papers was because he'd wanted her to be with him. To stay married. Which was ridiculous, because he *hated* marriage. And, as it turned out, he'd been right all along—marriage didn't work for him. Dahlia had proven it. After all they'd shared with each other, and after all the intimacy and passion they'd experienced together, after he'd confessed he *loved* her…she'd let him sign those damn papers anyway. He was refilling the shot glass when he heard footsteps behind him.

"Is this pity party a solo gig, or can I join in?" His father came out of the house and set another shot glass on the table. Rawlston filled it and nodded toward the empty chair.

"Suit yourself, but I'll warn you—I'm lousy company."

"Yeah, I figured that when I saw you sucking down whiskey this early in the day." Dad sat with a heavy sigh, staring out at the range. "Is it working?"

"Is *what* working?"

"Soaking yourself in booze. Is it dulling the pain? Has it solved any problems?" His father's tone was light and conversational, as if he was asking if Rawlston thought it might rain today.

"Not yet," he answered, downing the third shot and giving a satisfied sigh. "But I still have hope."

"Hope is good." Dad downed his shot, too, but slid the bottle out of Rawlston's reach to avoid an immediate refill. Then he set his shot glass down with a thunk. "But this isn't the way to get your girl back."

"I think that ship has sailed, Dad." He paused, confused. He hadn't talked to anyone since Dahlia watched him sign the papers that ended their marriage. "Wait... how did you know about Dahlia and me? You just got home."

His father was still staring out into the distance, watching Tripp chase a rabbit into a pile of brush. Happy with the thrill of the chase, the dog emerged from the brush without a rabbit, but with a happy bounce to his gait as his stubby tail wagged. Some of the cattle had come closer to the barns last night as a storm rolled through. Spotting the nearby cattle, Tripp trotted over, going under the fence and casually bringing the cows together in a group, working back and forth slowly. It was like he was practicing his herding skills without really trying to move the cattle.

Keith Ames gave a small shrug. "One person tells a friend who tells another friend who tells me. It's how small towns work, son."

Rawlston frowned. Who would have told a friend of Dad's? How many people knew, not only about their argument, but about their marriage? He thought about his conversation with Beau Weatherly at the reception. How Beau had just randomly brought up the topic of sheep and cattle grazing together. Rawlston didn't know how Beau had found out about him and Dahlia, but it was clear he had. And he *was* Dad's best friend.

"Marriage and me just don't get along, Dad. Never have, never will."

"That's a load of bull. Marriage, even the good ones, take work, son. You don't quit the first time you hit a speed bump. Not if you love each other. And I've got a hunch you two love each other quite a bit."

"I love her completely. I thought she felt the same way, but…well, I hurt her, and now she doesn't trust me. I've apologized over and over. I call. I text. Hell, I even sent her emails. I went to her house, but she wouldn't talk to me. She sent her twin out to tell me to leave. I left another voicemail just this morning. I even sent her roses…twice."

His father turned to stare at him, looking dumbfounded. "That sounds a touch desperate, don't you think? Give the woman time to think without you pestering her every hour."

Rawlston shook his head sharply, and immediately regretted it when everything went blurry. Maybe whiskey wasn't the solution after all. He swallowed hard, clearing his throat and trying to clear his head.

"I *am* desperate, Dad. She ended the marriage, and if I give her too much time, she might just end *us* for good. I can't sit back and let that happen. I have to *do* something." He slapped his hand on the table, making the empty shot glasses jump. "Why can't you see that?

I have to do something, or I might lose everything that matters to me."

"It was *doing something* that got you in trouble in the first place. Dahlia Fortune is an independent woman, maybe too much so, but that's who she is. That's who you fell in love with. Do you really think browbeating her is going to be effective? Is she the type of woman who responds to being nagged?"

"I'm not nagging her. I'm just… I'm being persistent." He winced. That was the same as nagging, and they both knew it. "But isn't that persistence proving to her that I want her back?"

"Maybe." Dad nodded thoughtfully. "Or maybe it's proving that you want to control her decisions. Isn't that why she got upset in the first place? Because you tried to take away her ability to make her own choices for herself?"

"That's not what…" His voice faded. "Oh, hell, that *is* what it probably feels like to her. I'm making the same mistake all over again. I'm making her hate me."

His father chuckled. "Slow down, boy. Let's not leap to extremes here. If she loves you, it'll be damn tough to turn that into hate. But you gotta give her time to breathe. You're worried that she doesn't trust you, but you have to trust *her* a little, too."

Tripp gave a light yip out beyond the fence. A cow and her calf had decided to leave the group, and Tripp dropped his head low and went to work to bring them back. He didn't charge at them. He got beyond them and started crossing back and forth, easing them in the direction he wanted.

"Look at that dog," Dad said. "Look how he's moving them, but without chasing them or stressing them out. He's left them an opening, and he's just hanging out, giving them a chance to *take* that opening. Instinctively, he trusts that old cow to know she and her baby belong with the herd. And watch, there she goes." The cow and calf trotted toward the others, with Tripp quietly zigzagging behind them. "That's what you need to do with Dahlia."

"I need to *herd* her?" Rawlston was teasing, and realized it felt good to laugh a little. It felt normal. Hopeful. His dad just rolled his eyes.

"No, you lunkhead. You just need to give her an open path back to you, then shut up and trust her to take it. Have some faith in the woman. If she loves you, she'll come around, once she nurses that hurt for a while." Dad took the whiskey bottle, but he only filled the shot glasses halfway. He held his up in a mock toast, and Rawlston returned the gesture as his father made his point. "Let her come back without being pushed, son."

An opening. The words rolled around in his head a few times, until an idea was born. He drank the whiskey, knowing that sip would be his last for a few days. He had work to do. He grinned at his father.

"Dad, you're a genius."

Chapter Nineteen

Dahlia was sitting with Hope and little Evie when she checked her phone and noticed she'd missed a text from Rawlston. They were on the shaded portion of Ridge's deck, after Dahlia had brought over a breakfast casserole to share. Hope still hadn't remembered much about her past, other than knowing that she'd been running from danger of some sort. But Dahlia had stopped by a few times, as Ridge suggested, and he was right about her liking the quiet woman and her sweet infant girl once she'd gotten to know them.

Her brother had gone to the ranch office after breakfast, and the women had decided to enjoy some fresh air while the temperatures were still on the cooler side. Evie was sound asleep in the baby carrier Ridge had bought for her.

"Is everything okay?" Hope asked, frowning at the phone in Dahlia's hand. "Is that bad news?"

"I'm not really sure *what* it is."

It had been two days since Rawlston's last text, where he'd promised to back off and give her time. That he'd be waiting for as long as it took, but he wouldn't bother her anymore. She couldn't help wondering who had talked to him about his barrage of messages after their argument.

Whoever it was, she was grateful to them. It had been easier to think without him trying so hard. But here he was, texting again. He wasn't asking her to do anything this time, though. Not talk to him. Not forgive him. He was just telling her something that made no sense.

I'll be up by the cottonwood tree this morning working on a project you might want to see. If you'd rather see it alone, I'll be done around noontime.

Was he asking to meet her? If so, why was he so careful to let her know when he *wouldn't* be there? Her pulse jumped. Rawlston did it because he wanted to give her options. He was opening the door, but not forcing his way through it. Not pulling her through, either.

She bit down on her lower lip, still mulling it over. What *project* was he working on up there? Had the sheep gotten through his fence again? Maybe he'd added the lower strand of wire he'd mentioned to keep them out, despite his concern that they'd crawl under it anyway. Why was he making it a mystery?

Then Dahlia smiled. Fortunes loved their mysteries. He was teasing her with just enough information to make her curious. He knew her so well. Her smile deepening, she checked her watch. He'd sent this text an hour ago, but she'd set her phone aside while they were eating breakfast and hadn't seen it.

"Um, Hope, I'm sorry, but—"

"You have to go." Hope nodded. "I figured from that big smile on your face that I haven't seen much this week. Go on. We'll catch up later."

They hugged and Dahlia hurried to her golf cart, then

down to her stables. She was in capris and canvas flats with a ruffled gauzy top—not exactly riding clothes. She didn't even have a hat. She wasn't going to take the time to change.

Once she'd made the decision to try to meet with Rawlston, her heart was thumping so hard in her chest that she could almost hear it pounding out *Hurry! Hurry!* She pulled Rebel from his stall, forcing herself to slow enough that she wouldn't upset the stallion. Meanwhile, the clock was ticking in her head. It was almost noon.

Rawlston had put the invitation out there, and she was finally ready to make the move toward a future together. He'd made a mistake. A couple of them, actually. But once her sense of betrayal had cooled, she'd realized her mother was right. She was clinging to her anger to protect herself from being hurt again, without considering that he was sincerely remorseful and deserved a second chance. She'd want one from him if she'd been the one to make a mistake.

If they loved each other, they'd probably be giving each other lots of second chances through the years. She felt a warm thrill at the thought of years together with Rawlston. It was worth risking occasional hot tempers if it meant spending a lifetime with the man. They could handle it. *Love* could handle it.

Luckily, it was overcast, keeping the air cool enough that she didn't have to worry about stressing her horse physically. Once he was saddled, Rebel was ready for a run. She made him wait until they were in the main range before giving him his head. The stallion actually hesitated for a moment, unsure what to do. She'd very rarely just let him run. Once he realized she meant it, he took off like a bullet, racing across the meadow. She spotted the sheep on the far side of the hill, and, even though they were far away, they still scattered at the sight of the big horse charging toward them.

Rawlston was there. Or at least, *Malloy* was there, grazing under the wide cottonwood. So Rawlston had to be nearby. She reined in Rebel as they approached the summit. He was blowing hard, prancing sideways and snorting as Malloy raised his head and let out a whinny. That's when Rawlston straightened over near the gate.

Wait. Where did that *gate* come from? The only gate between their properties was down at the bottom of the far side of the hill. She and Rawlston had joked about adding a gate that would make his rides to her house shorter. He watched as she pulled up and slid off Rebel. He arched a brow at her shoes.

"Not exactly safe footwear for riding—especially *that* kind of riding." He watched as she patted Rebel's neck. "You gave the big boy a good run. In a hurry to get somewhere?"

He still hadn't moved from his spot by the gate. What was he waiting for? He'd given her the opportunity, but now she realized it was up to her to make the final move. She tucked her horse's reins through her belt loop. With these linen capris, it wouldn't take more than Rebel shaking his head to rip the loop loose, but his training held. The stallion wasn't interested in testing her today. Trusting her, the same way Rawlston was.

Seeing him so close was all she needed to chase away any remaining doubts. Tall, sweaty, handsome. Eyes full of worry and love. He took off his hat and wiped his brow with his handkerchief. Watching her. Waiting for her to come to him. She led Rebel forward a few steps so she could move into Rawlston's arms. He wrapped her in an embrace so tight it almost took her breath away, and they stood like that for a long time, just clinging to each other. It had only been days, but it felt like years since he'd held her. Kissed her, like he was doing now. Hard. Deep. Desperate.

When he finally pulled away, they were both breathing heavily. He turned slightly and gestured toward the gate.

"I was an idiot, Dahlia. I should have fought for you instead of signing those damn papers. And then I kept pressuring you instead of trusting you. I love you, sweetheart, and I'm opening my heart, just like I've opened this fence line. No more fear. No more doubt. No more lies, I promise. Never again…"

"No more lies," Dahlia repeated, kissing the corner of his mouth. "No more fear. No doubts. I like the sound of that." She moved to kiss him again, but he stepped back.

She was confused until he gestured to the other change he'd made to the fence. The sections on either side of the gate had been reconfigured. He hadn't added a third strand to block the sheep. Instead, he'd raised the second strand right in the middle, so there was now plenty of room for her sheep to walk through to his range.

"I don't understand," she said. "I thought the idea was to keep sheep *out*. Aren't you worried about your cattle?"

"Turns out I was wrong about more things than just marriage. I've since been educated on the facts about sheep and cattle sharing ranges. And it actually can work. We'll just have to check to be sure your whole herd doesn't cross over. Kinda like marriage, it requires the right balance." He pulled her in for another kiss. "A little cooperation." He kissed her again. "A little com-promise." Another kiss. "Patience."

She chuckled. "You'll probably need that patience more than me."

He nodded and kissed her again. They were both so hungry for each other. "That's okay. I'm sure there are things you'll have to be patient about, too." He stepped back, then dropped to one knee, reaching for his pocket.

What. Is. Happening?

He pulled out a small box and opened it.

"Marry me, Dahlia. Again. For real."

Inside the box were two familiar wedding bands and a diamond ring. The rings from Las Vegas. He gave her a bright grin, his eyes shining, with only the slightest touch of guilt showing.

"I couldn't return them, babe. Somehow, I already knew that our marriage was for keeps." He shrugged. "Well, maybe not *that* marriage, since we annulled it, but—"

She dropped to her knees in front of him, ignoring his surprise. Her hands clutched his fingers, which were holding the box and rings between the two of them. She was laughing, giddy with relief and joy.

"You're not the only one with a confession to make." His forehead furrowed, and she placed her hand on his cheek. "I never sent those silly papers to the attorneys. I shredded them the day after we argued. No matter what happened, I wanted us to make the decision about our future calmly, not in anger. And frankly, I knew in my heart that I didn't want our marriage to be over, either."

He stared, then took her hand from his face and kissed her palm, smiling against her skin. "So it appears neither one of us can be trusted to end this marriage."

She nodded. They were still on their knees, facing each other. "Something else we have in common. Loving each other."

He leaned forward, looking deep into her eyes until she felt him touching her soul. "I will love you forever, Dahlia. With all my heart. I don't ever *not* want to be married to you." He slid the band and the diamond onto her finger, then watched as she put his wedding band on his hand. The rings looked like they belonged there. "I'll be a real husband this time, and no more secrets. All that drama is for Fortunes, and you're an Ames now. I can't wait to tell the world."

"I love you, too, Rawlston. With all my heart. Maybe it was fate that made that bratty kid pour so much vodka in our fruit punch that night."

He laughed, kissed her again, then looked over her shoulder. "Uh, your killer horse seems to be bored with us."

She looked back in surprise. Rebel must have pulled his rein from her belt loop without her even noticing. Or maybe it came free by itself when she dropped to her knees with Rawlston. Either way, the paint horse was grazing calmly about ten feet away, between them and Malloy. Neither horse seemed the least bit interested in each other or their humans.

She and Rawlston stood slowly, and she moved closer to Rebel until she was able to take up the reins. He lifted his head and bumped it against her, then went back to grazing.

"Well, I'll be. A good gallop was exactly what he needed," she said, patting his shoulder.

Rawlston walked up and slid his arms around her. "Or maybe he's a romantic at heart, and we charmed him."

She leaned back against his chest, laughing softly. "I think my theory is more likely."

A few of the sheep had wandered closer, and Rawlston gave a short command. She hadn't even noticed Tripp sleeping in the tall grass by the tree. He was awake now, watching the sheep intently. But he didn't move.

"That poor dog's going to be very confused when he can't chase sheep anymore."

"He's a quick learner. Besides, maybe we'll put him to use herding sheep on *your* side of the fence."

"You mean *our* side." She pulled away, but held on to his hand. "We're married for real now, so there is no more yours and mine. Which means…" She tapped under his chin with her fingers teasingly. "That *you* are now a sheep farmer."

"And you—" he tugged her close "—are the prettiest damn cattle rancher in Texas." He nipped at her ear, his words sending shivers across her skin. "A cattle rancher I really want to make love to right now. I've missed having you in my arms."

"My place is…" She grinned. "I mean, *our* lake house is closer."

He chuckled. "The attorneys are going to have fun with all of this, aren't they? But I agree that heading to the lake house is a good idea. *Right now.*"

They both mounted and headed down the hill, hand in hand. Rebel had pinned his ears at Malloy's closeness at first, but then begrudgingly settled into walking at his side. The ride was slow and easy. Comfortable.

Dahlia could picture them making this same ride thirty, forty, maybe fifty years from now. Coming down the hill to their home together. The barns were in sight when Rawlston spoke again.

"I know we're legally already married, but I want to give you a real wedding and a reception. Pick a date… maybe in the spring when everything is in bloom. It's my favorite time of the year in Texas. We'll renew our vows and party like we're still in high school."

"Spring sounds perfect," she agreed, remembering one more thing. "And I know exactly what my 'something old' will be." She waited until he looked over at her before she continued. "I just happen to have a long, sparkly wedding veil that lights up, if you can believe it. I'm sure it's a style that will be all the rage in Texas by next spring." He barked out a laugh as she continued. "It was something else I couldn't part with from Vegas."

He was still laughing as he leaned toward her, making Rebel unhappy enough to pin his ears again. Rawlston paid him no mind.

"Am I also something that you won't part with from Vegas?"

"You were by far the best thing I got on my trip to Las Vegas, Mr. Ames. I'm not about to give you up."

"That's good news, Mrs. Ames, because I feel the same way. Vegas was very good to us."

"I agree." They reined in the horses at the stable, dismounting and quickly moving into each other's arms. He traced a trail of kisses down her neck until she sighed. "If I had to wake up married to someone in Las Vegas," she whispered in his ear, "I'm very glad that someone was you."

* * * * *

Don't miss
Nine Months to a Fortune
by New York Times bestselling author
Elizabeth Bevarly,
the next installment in the new continuity
The Fortunes of Texas: Fortune's Secret Children
On sale September 2024, wherever Harlequin
books and ebooks are sold!